DETOURS

DETOURS

Plus Five Short Stories

Neil Stipp

iUniverse, Inc.
New York   Bloomington

Detours
(A novella)

iUniverse books may be ordered through booksellers or by contacting:

iUniverse
1663 Liberty Drive
Bloomington, IN 47403
www.iuniverse.com
1-800-Authors (1-800-288-4677)

ISBN: 978-1-4401-9718-5 (sc)
ISBN: 978-1-4401-9719-2 (ebk)

Printed in the United States of America

iUniverse rev. date: 12/16/2009

Contents

Foreword

The short novel *Detours*, and the short stories that follow, involve people in conflicting relationships and forces. They experience the realistic emotions of jealousy, passion, euphoria, guilt, vindictiveness, gratification, to name a few. The plots detail how they live out these emotions, and the end result that ensues. My only goal for writing this book is to entertain, and to make the reader's journey from the current world to the world of fiction an enjoyable one. If you take away something meaningful from the pages that follow, then it's an extra plus for both of us. So sit back, relax and enjoy!

DETOURS

1

Brandon stretched as he awoke from his nap on the jet airliner and pulled a muscle. He let out a loud groan and reached for his calf. It was not the first time this had occurred, having frequently gone through the same experience recently in his bed at home.

"Again?" said his wife, Rose, sitting next to him and sounding more agitated than sympathetic.

Some of the passengers heard the groan and turned their heads, and a stewardess stood over him. "Are you all right, sir?"

"Pulled a muscle—again," he said, continuing to rub his calf. "I suppose I should see a doctor about it, some day. Happens all the time."

"He needs to exercise, is what he needs to do," said Rose. "Strengthen his muscles."

"Thanks for your compassion," Brandon retorted. The stewardess left, and the interested passengers returned to their individual activities.

Brandon and Rose were flying to Hawaii from Los Angeles for a seven-day vacation on a last-ditch effort to save their marriage. It was the advice of their marriage counselor, claiming the couple was not spending enough time alone, burdened by work, kids, and individual activities in their everyday lives which prevented them from getting away.

Their twenty-year wedding anniversary "celebrated" two months prior had been an absolute dud, and reminded them of happier and exciting times years ago. Exchanging cards was all that could be mustered on that special day. Their counselor questioned why they couldn't have gone out to dinner, with the response being that both would get on each other's nerves in no time. The sex life was gone, and intimacy of any kind was at a premium. This vacation was the final hope of resurrecting the fire and marital bliss that characterized the opening years of their relationship—years that produced four children, and comments, such as "they are the ideal couple," from their friends.

"I want some red wine," Brandon said softly to himself.

"That will definitely help your calf," Rose responded.

"Your sense of humor has been in decline since our honeymoon. Can it get any worse?"

"Can your lack of exercise get any worse? I've told you to work out in the gym with me. You sit at that desk all day long, and some of your muscles haven't been used in weeks. You would feel much better, Brandon, and you wouldn't be pulling a muscle every other time you move." Rose gave a big sigh, shifted her weight, and went back to reading her book.

"Could I have some red wine, please?" he asked a stewardess walking by. "I know we land in twenty minutes."

"I'm sure we can accommodate you in a couple of minutes."

Brandon thought of the times he had been in Hawaii. Their honeymoon, then the time a year ago when they visited their oldest daughter who was in college, and the time ten years ago when he and Rose visited friends and did some hiking and helicopter riding on Kauai, and . . . oh yes, how could he have forgotten?

His favorite summer ever, the summer of 1961, and Cassie Logan. His first love whom he met in college. Spending the entire summer in her Honolulu apartment. Breaking up with her at the end of the summer, or actually, she breaking it off with him. His most satisfying and romantic summer, until the end. Cassie getting married months later after he returned to California, and breaking his heart. Being in deep depression for weeks until he met Rose in the most unbelievable way, and then not being able to think of anything but *her*. Falling in love with Rose, and having Cassie diminish from his thoughts. The marriage to Rose within a year. The first child, Brandy, within a year after that. The irrepressible joy of married life. The new home, three more kids, success with the new job. The perfect life. And then, within a few years it was gone. He looked over at Rose reading her book. She was a woman he no longer knew. She was a different person than whom he married—almost a stranger.

He was going to see Cassie in Hawaii this time. It had been twenty-two years since he had seen her. Rose wouldn't know about it. Brandon got her address and phone number through a phone book. He found out her marriage lasted only about a year and she had a son who would be twenty-one now. Was Cassie pregnant when she married? Had she wanted to contact him over the years but didn't because of his marriage? The previous times he was in Hawaii, Brandon had thought of reaching her, but resisted the temptation. But now, his marriage was irrelevant. He was on this trip partially to convince Rose and the counselor that he made an attempt to save the relationship—but he really wanted to see Cassie again.

He received his wine, and drank half of his glass. The whole thing was ironic—to see Cassie on the same trip that was meant to keep him with Rose. What did he want the most? He had dreamed of the restoration of his marriage, but he had been dreaming for years and now he had the opportunity of seeing his first love again. He remembered the dialogue with her on the phone a week ago:

"This is a voice from the past, Cassie."

"Good God. Have no idea."

"Really? You sound great."

"Thanks. Who is this, really? I need to know or I'll hang up."

"We last spoke twenty-two years ago. That was what? Was it 1961?"

"Hmm, 1961. What in God's name was I doing in 1961?"

"You were living in an apartment in Honolulu."

"That's right! Now let's see. I . . . oh, my gosh. It can't be. Brandon?"

"It's me."

"What on earth are you doing? How are you?"

"Still thinking of my first love."

"You were always such a charmer. Where are you?"

"In the L.A. area. I'm coming to Hawaii next week." Brandon stopped, and then took a deep breath. "I want to see you."

There was silence on the other end of the line. The silence felt longer to Brandon than what it really was. "O.K. All right. Sure! I would like to see you again. Really! I thought you were married . . . still."

"I'm . . . coming to Hawaii because of business. How did you know of my marriage?"

"College friends, you know. Word gets around. Do you remember Donna James?"

"Donna James. Yes, yes I do."

"She told me she saw you at a bowling alley, and you two talked."

"O.K."

"Where'd you get my number?" she asked.

"Phone book from a library. You took back your maiden name. I've known where you've been for years."

They continued to talk for a good fifteen minutes. Brandon had to lie only once more, and it was about his divorce. When the dialogue ended, he felt twenty years younger. His soul felt revived, his passion for living took a startling turn, and he felt like a new man. But when and how will he be able to see her with Rose on the trip?

He finished his wine and felt the jet airliner descend for landing.

"Finished," said Rose, closing her book.

"With what?"

"My collection of short stories. Started reading them just three days ago. Don't worry. I have plenty of magazines to read on the beach. How's your calf?"

It was four in the afternoon when they got off the plane. They each received their lei and got their luggage in no time. The older Brandon became, the more he had learned to travel lightly.

Heading toward the rent-a-car office, Brandon's calf had only a slight throb and he walked with a mild limp. Rose's mood took a leap for the better as the island seemed to make her look and feel happier. The glow in her face was noticeable to Brandon, and perhaps Hawaii had helped her remember the honeymoon, as well as the exciting times they always had when returning to the islands. Brandon continued looking at her, and Rose gave a quick smile back at him, and then turned her face toward the sky as if to soak in the warmth from the sun.

The drive to the hotel took only fifteen minutes, and when Brandon opened the drapes in their hotel suite and saw the Pacific Ocean in all her glory, he let out a gasp of euphoria. There were a few seconds when his mind was totally blank of any negativity or despair and all he could feel was peaceful tranquility. The ocean reminded him of a rendezvous in paradise, and he received an instant hot flash.

"Oh, baby," said Rose softly. "How beautiful." Brandon decided to reach out and hug Rose and noticed she was already reaching for him as well. They embraced, and then Brandon embraced her tighter and noticed she was breathing heavier. He turned and looked into her blue eyes and kissed her quickly, and then Rose, who was eight inches shorter, turned her head and rested it on his chest, purring like a kitten.

They said nothing for five minutes but continued embracing as Brandon dreamed that time would just stop and he could be in this position for eternity. Then everything would be all right. He would need nothing else. Why couldn't the marriage always be like this? This was unusual, and he also knew this moment could not last. Hunger would set in after a few hours, or they would eventually need to get their rest or use the bathroom.

Rose looked back up at Brandon and said, "This is so peaceful. I love the ocean. Don't you?"

"Of course."

Then Brandon broke the embrace and jumped on to the bed nearby. He bounced a couple of times and Rose laughed. Then she, too, jumped on to the bed and cuddled next to him. He felt drowsy, partly because of the wine, but mostly because of the feeling of being away from his troubles at work and soaking in the different environment. He dozed off, and Rose, with her head resting on his chest, did the same.

2

Brandon stretched in his sleep and pulled another calf muscle that caused him to awake and groan loudly. He woke up Rose as well, as he got out of bed and tried to walk it off. "Damn," he muttered. "Damn it." He opened the sliding door to the balcony porch and slumped into a chair. It was about six o'clock in the evening and the cool breeze felt good to his face, and he had a sunset over the ocean to look forward to. He didn't need to move—he would just relax. Rose brought him some coffee five minutes later.

"Thanks, babe," he said in a monotone.

"This will be a good evening. Clear skies now. Sunset should be in an hour," she said, as she caressed his back.

"I know. When do you think we should see Brandy?" he asked, in reference to their first-born daughter.

"I don't care. Any time is fine," she replied.

Brandy was at the University of Hawaii studying journalism, and had just finished her sophomore year. She was given her name as a minor adjustment to the name Brandon Jr. when she was born as a girl rather than the boy her parents had thought would come.

He shifted his weight. "We should call and let her know we've arrived. She's expecting us, you know."

"I hope you'll be more favorable company than last year."

"I don't want a lecture. I thought that boyfriend she had was probably shacking up with her, and I got uneasy." He sighed. "I remained compatible."

"I don't think you were. You acted nervous when you met him, and you didn't look him in the eye when you shook hands. It makes people think you don't care."

"Care about what?"

"About them."

"Well, I certainly didn't come over there to her apartment to find out that her boyfriend was probably shacking up with her."

"But we still don't know that he was. We never found out, remember?"

"So we're to give her the benefit of the doubt because she's our daughter. That's what you're going to say next, right?"

"Don't presume what I'm going to say," she said coldly.

"O.K., then we need to presume that our daughter has Trojan condoms in the bathroom drawer to be handed out to any beau who comes her way, is that it? Those condoms I saw weren't really her boyfriend's . . . what's his name, Ron? They weren't really his then."

"Maybe they weren't."

"Regardless, it's bad news either way. Either she likes to screw off with other men in her apartment which is why she had the condoms, or they belong to Ron who lives there. Which is worse?"

"I don't know, and I don't care," Rose said, irritatingly.

"You don't care? You're her mother."

She hesitated, and then said: "Oh, of course I care. But . . . what in the world were you doing looking in a drawer of her bathroom anyway?"

"Looking for some aspirin. I didn't see it in the medicine cabinet."

"You never take aspirin. You know it doesn't help you."

"Damn, I hate this conversation," he retorted. "Well, it didn't take us long, did it?   Here we are in Hawaii, sitting on a balcony overlooking the ocean near Waikiki, and we are already arguing."

"We aren't arguing," she said softly, with a change in tone.

"We are!"   He sipped his coffee and set it down hard.

"About what?"

"About . . . Brandy and her boyfriend and whether he lives with her."

"You brought it up. I didn't."

"But you brought up Brandy."

"No I didn't. You brought up Brandy."

"I did? No I didn't. Oh. Well, you brought up the fact I should act more favorable to her."

"And I hope you will. We only see her once a year, and, at this point, it is more important to me that we be supportive of her than suspicious."

"I'm not suspicious," Brandon said. "I know that her boyfriend is in there with her."

"O.K. maybe he is," Rose said calmly.

"Well, I can't be supportive of that."

"But you can be supportive of other things relating to our daughter."

"I don't want a lecture from you," said Brandon, raising his voice almost to a shout. "I'm tired of arguing about it." He took another sip and set the cup down hard.

"You're arguing with yourself.   I would appreciate it if you would be more supportive of Brandy this time. That's all I wish to say, and I'm going to drop the subject and not say anymore. I'm done." She went back in the suite.

"You always get the last word," he said. Brandon realized again he needed to say less and less to Rose if he was going to survive this vacation. Why did everything with her start so well and end so poorly, including sex and dialogue? He felt no affection for her at this time, either mental or physical. It was great less than two hours ago when they embraced and didn't say anything.

They did manage to call their daughter on the phone and set up a time for them to get together at her apartment at eleven the next morning. Both were enthused.

A few minutes later they were walking on the shore, having the soft waves touch their feet. The sun was setting, and Brandon and Rose enjoyed hearing only nature: the birds chirping and the sound of the waves. Brandon thought of speaking about something and then caught himself—it would only lead to an argument in about five minutes. He wasn't about to spoil the beauty seen before him. It was nice that Rose kept herself in shape and could stay up with his moderately fast gait, he thought to himself. He never had to slow down for her.

"The breeze feels so refreshing I could stay out here all evening," Rose said suddenly.

Brandon merely nodded, continuing to have his arm around Rose while walking briskly. Rose is nice to look at, and so is the scenery, he thought. We could share our joy together by merely observing things of grandeur and beauty. That would keep us together a while longer. Dialogue is bad for us and only leads to controversy.

Finally he stopped his walking and turned directly out at the ocean. Rose was facing him with her head just below his chin. He clasped her hands in his, feeling those earthy yet fragile hands that he had held twenty years ago when he said "I do." It brought back the memory in a flash. Then he let go of them and embraced her, with her head turned sideways on his chest.

"You know, I feel . . ." Rose started to say.

"Don't speak," he said abruptly.

Rose remained next to his chest so it was not possible for Brandon to see her reaction to his remark. He could feel Rose's heavy breathing with his hands embracing her. They both could only hear the waves now. If he could only stay in this position forever of feeling Rose and seeing the ocean, he could be permanently happy. But, again, time would not stop for him.

He saw a dove glide downward toward the water as the sun disappeared below the horizon.

3

They called Brandy the next morning and agreed that eleven o'clock would be the time to get together at her apartment. On their drive over to see her, Brandon was trying to figure out how he could steal away from his wife later in the day to see Cassie. It was not worrisome yet because it was only Sunday and they were to stay in Hawaii until Saturday. Perhaps he could get Rose to go on a shopping spree, and then get away by telling her he would like to see a realtor or something. Cassie worked in a bank as a teller, and Brandon knew exactly what bank and where it was because of a street map. Rose remained motionless and quiet during Brandon's thought process.

The couple greeted Brandy with enthusiasm. She seemed more nervous than when they last saw her. No one else was living with her as far as they could detect. Brandon was dedicated to remaining pleasant regardless of what he might find out about her love-life.

Rose excused herself to the restroom after only ten minutes. Brandy saw this as a breakthrough to her dad.

"Why are you even thinking about divorcing mom?" she asked her dad in a quiet, whispering tone, so that her mom couldn't hear. "Mom told me on the phone that this so-called 'vacation' was actually prescribed by your marriage counselor to get your act back together again and relive the good-old days? Is that true? Is this what it takes?"

Brandon thought before he spoke. He spoke very softly but focused. "There's quite a bit you don't know about your mother. I've tried. I really have. We can't have a dialogue without arguing sooner or later. She's a bore at parties. She doesn't want to do the things I want to do." He was going to say more, than stopped. Brandy listened intently.

"Do you realize how much you would hurt me if you two split? I'm not a child, but I am nineteen and it would still hurt me a great deal.

And if it could hurt me at my age, how much more would it hurt Jana, Lester, and James?"

"I've thought about the kids and how much it might hurt them. Don't you think I've thought of that?"

"I think you're only thinking of yourself," she said louder, which prompted a "sh" from her dad as he looked toward the restroom.

"Listen. Your mom can act . . . can act like a bitch sometimes and it's hard for me to put up with it. And she hasn't even started menopause yet."

"What are you searching for? What is it? You may go through a rough time now, but won't it smooth over?"

"You're majoring in journalism not psychology. You've never spoken to me like this before." He realized for the first time that his oldest daughter was truly an adult now.

"You two have never thought about splitting up before. I've bragged to my friends about you two and what a wonderful family we have. I would be devastated." Brandon looked closely into the eyes of his daughter and he saw desperation. It was a hopeless, sad, and frantic look. This was going to be even harder to go through than what he first realized. He and Rose would bring devastation to this family.

"I don't know what to tell you, Brandy," he said forlornly. He shook his head slightly, and then put it in his hands. Then he looked up at her again. "You don't know what I've been through."

"Whatever you're searching for can be found in mom. You just need to look closer for it. It's there. I'm sure mom still loves you. She still speaks fondly of you over the phone."

"She hasn't told me she loves me in awhile. You . . ." Brandon stopped and decided he would say no more. He was going to mention *his* hurt last year when he saw the condoms in Brandy's bathroom, but couldn't get himself to say it to her face. It was something he would probably need to write to her about. Brandon saw his daughter now look at him with disgust.

"You're still too young to understand these types of things," he quickly said impulsively.

"I'm an adult."

"But you're still too young to understand these things." He paused, and then caught a glimmer of hope. "Besides, we haven't filed. Not yet. We may never. Things may straighten out."

"Let's hope so."

Rose returned from the restroom and the conversation reverted to the previous topic before she left.

"Your pictures are perfect for this room, Brandy," Rose said in a spirited manner. "Did you buy them at an art gallery?"

"Yes. Here in Honolulu."

"Weren't they expensive?"

"Very. But I wanted the living room to at least look elegant. Well, did you bring your swimming suits? I hope so. The pool is warm."

"Yes we did," said Brandon. He stood up. "I think I could use a good swim. Any jacuzzi, or just a pool?"

"Just a pool. There's a jacuzzi at the Y down the street two blocks."

"That's O.K. A pool right now would be perfect." Anything would be fine for Brandon as long as he was not alone with his daughter lecturing him. "Ready for the pool, Rose?"

"I am. There are dressing rooms outside next to the pool?" she asked.

Brandy nodded. "Yes. The gate is locked to get to the pool, but here's an extra key."

❦   ❦   ❦

"Is dad's work affecting him?" Brandy asked her mother by the pool. Brandon was in the dressing room getting back into his regular clothes after his swim.

"He has no chance for any promotion or raise now," Rose responded. "He's maxed out. They have a cap on the salary for his position. So he just goes in there and works hard in order to keep the job he has."

"I can't believe that you two are near the end of your rope. Why do you want to throw away your marriage?"

"We wouldn't be throwing away anything, really. The marriage has had its good moments, and you kids have been the sparkplugs. Nothing is wasted. But we irritate each other now. I don't know why. If I knew, I would fix it. There's no one simple answer to things like this. Perhaps something can happen this week when we're in a relaxing mode that will give us a jump start. Boy, we need one."

The two remained silent for awhile. Brandy started to say something, and then stopped. Brandon came out of the dressing room and went into the apartment. He got some ginger-ale from the refrigerator and sat down on the sofa in the living room. He thought of turning on the television, but instead decided to solely concentrate on how he could see Cassie this week without Rose knowing. Just to get away from Rose for awhile would require some ingenuity. Was she going to do everything with him? She knows he doesn't like to shop, and perhaps he could check out a museum in another part of town by himself. That might work. He would need to see Cassie during the day. Rose would get too suspicious if he got up at midnight from bed and told her he needed to go out for a walk because he couldn't sleep. Brandon's heart almost took an exciting extra beat knowing that he might see Cassie in less than twenty-four hours.

He looked out to see Rose and Brandy talking intensely. Brandy continued to look extremely nervous. How much did Rose divulge to Brandy over the phone about the impending breakup? He figured they had been talking over this matter perhaps for weeks. Brandy was taking it too hard. He felt a tinge of sympathy for her, and it hit him in the pit of his stomach. But he didn't feel he was entirely to blame. Watching the two out on the porch was like watching charades. Rose put her hands on either side of her face and bowed her head as if she couldn't bear to hear more, while it appeared Brandy was raising her voice at her mother. Brandon thought about going out to calm things down for the sake of feeling sorry for Rose and to stop Brandy from saying something she might be sorry for later. He discarded this notion, and turned on the television to watch baseball. Perhaps Brandy needs to get out of her all of this pent up emotion that has been building over the last few weeks. The Cubs were playing the Dodgers. He thought about his three younger kids and whether they could sense what was happening to the marriage. Will the Dodgers go to the bullpen to hold on to their 4-2 lead or stay with their starter? Should he and Rose wait until their last child turns eighteen before filing for divorce? Their youngest, James, is thirteen now. Could they both wait that long? Yes, the Dodgers are going to their bullpen. Brandon thought it would hurt the youngest the most, but maybe it was the opposite. Is Brandy taking it so hard because she has the closest family ties? The Cubs have the tying runs on base with no outs. Brandon couldn't concentrate and turned off the television, as his mind was consumed on the week at hand, and Cassie. He knew the decisions made in the next few hours would influence the rest of his life, and his family's.

Brandon wanted a beer and walked to the refrigerator but didn't find any liquor, and remembered Brandy was not at the drinking age yet. He would have plenty of time this week to drink and sat down again on the sofa. Brandon almost dozed off when Rose and Brandy walked back in the apartment after about twenty minutes.

"Did you two get it all straightened out?" Brandon inquired.

"Fat chance," replied Brandy.

Rose sighed deeply, took a quick glance at Brandon and then turned away.

Brandy prepared lunch for her mom and dad, then they ate with so little conversation that an onlooker would have thought each person was a mute. Rose tried to think of a subject to talk about, but weakened in her attempts when she realized any other subject would come across as a way to avoid the all-pervasive issue. She would need to talk more to Brandy when her husband wasn't around. Brandon was too hungry to bother with talking, and when the meal was finished he left with Rose, kissing his daughter and wishing her the best.

🍁   🍁   🍁

"We could have stayed longer," Rose said, as they were driving back to the hotel. Brandon didn't reply.

"She acted as if we should stay longer," Rose continued. "But she was so stressed I think it would have been uncomfortable for both us. Did you sense her desperation?"

"Yes, I did. If we could have shifted the subject to other things instead of talking about ourselves and our problems, it would have been better."

"She's going to therapy because of us."

"What?" Brandon sat up in his car seat instead of slouching. "Therapy! That costs a lot of money. How often?"

"Once a week for an hour," Rose answered. "She's felt depressed and needed to talk to someone."

"But, doesn't she have friends? Of course she does. They're free. She should be talking to her friends if she's depressed. She's making too much of this. She's an adult, off on her own. It's not like she's living with us, and needs to bear with a troubled relationship every day."

"You always make light of everything, Brandon. Her problem is that we were a source of stability for her years ago and she's seeing it crumble. She remembers the Christmas mornings when we were such a happy family together, the vacations, the times we went camping. Family was a big thing to her, and she is seeing it deteriorate. Don't you understand that?"

Brandon and Rose lay on the beach at Waikiki later in the afternoon but didn't get much of a tan because of the clouds. Brandon enjoyed how the ocean felt and enjoyed splashing Rose who thought it was too cold when she went in with him. They had a very good dialogue on their beach blanket and both wondered why it continued so long without an argument. They concluded it was either due to the subjects they were talking about, or the ocean which was sending some magical vibes giving peace to their frame of mind.

4

The following day, Monday, was overcast as clouds were hovering over Honolulu, ready to breakthrough with some showers. After being compatible at breakfast together, Brandon was complaining that Rose was trying too hard to keep things at ease between themselves rather than acting herself. Rose accused Brandon of not trying hard *enough*. They agreed to go shopping after lunch in the city.

At two o'clock during their shopping, Brandon had a brainstorm. "I saw a camera shop about two blocks back there," he said. "Would like to spend some time in it."

"Why?"

"Just wanted to look at some cameras. I could use a smaller one. Why don't you go do more of your shopping and I could meet you at three at this corner. How 'bout it?"

Rose thought for awhile and gave him a strange stare. "I guess it would be all right. An hour?"

"Yes, that will give me plenty of time," Brandon said as he started heading the opposite direction.

"O.K., I guess. This corner?"

Brandon nodded and then started to walk swiftly. He arrived at the camera shop, spending only a couple of minutes inside, then immediately headed for the bank Cassie worked.

His heart was close to skipping a beat as the excitement pulsated within him. He walked into the bank and it was not busy. He looked at the teller line and didn't recognize Cassie at first. Then he looked at the only blonde again and came up closer to her. Yes, that was her, and he remembered that females usually age faster. It had been twenty-two years but it still caught Brandon totally off guard. Why does aging need to be part of the human experience? He had always remembered Cassie as a twenty-one year old. She had more wrinkles and gained more weight than Brandon had prepared for. The youthful gleam in her eyes was gone. Brandon came up to her spot in the teller line.

"Hello, Cassie?"

"Yes, may I help you?"

"I'm Brandon Peeters."

Her mouth opened wide. She gasped, and then put her hands to the side of her face. "Oh, my God!"

"How are you? Have you had lunch?"

"Yes, I just came back from lunch about twenty minutes ago." She had the same voice—the voice he remembered on the telephone. But her appearance had changed considerably. "Gracious, you look good," she said. "You've put on weight. You've really filled out." Brandon had hoped his change over the years had been for the better. He was about to say that his wife's cooking was responsible for the weight gain, but quickly caught himself. He didn't want to bring Rose into anything, and remembered he had told Cassie on the telephone he was in Hawaii on business.

"I don't have another break for about forty-five minutes," Cassie said.

"Well, I can't stay for quite that long. Perhaps we can see each other tonight for a bit. You live close by, don't you?"

"Fifteen minute drive, just outside Honolulu." She could see that a customer was now waiting. "I have time tonight. I'm taking classes at the University of Hawaii, a couple of night classes, but tonight I'm free." She smiled, and took out a piece of paper and began drawing directions quickly. The customer went to another teller. Brandon watched her hand and fingers as she wrote methodically. Her hand motions were the same as he had remembered. "And here's my phone and address."

"I'll try to see you tonight. Really, I will. I want to see you, badly. It has been a long time." There was a sense of anxiety in Brandon's voice that he didn't want to hear. He didn't want to make Cassie nervous, but her expression did not change.

"How long are you in Hawaii for your business?"

"Until this Saturday," he said, taking the paper from her. "You're still cute," Brandon said in a different voice—more reflective, and nostalgic.

"So are you," she said after a pause, and then she dropped her eyes.

"Well, you're going to have customers, so I'll let you go."

"Please call first if you decide you can come over."

"I'll try to make it tonight if I can. Bye." He reached out and touched her hand. She touched his hand firmly, and the handshake was without the shake. Then, Brandon recalled everything that was sexual about her. Cassie's touch had not changed. How he loved her touch. She was not nearly as attractive in her forties but the touch kept him in focus of how attracted he used to be to her. Maybe, over time, he would adjust in his mind how she now looked and fall in love with her all over again. He left the bank quickly, and began to figure out how he could possibly see Cassie that night when he was going to be spending at least most of the evening with Rose at a luau.

He got back to the corner at three where he was to meet Rose, and she was nowhere around. She finally arrived at almost three-thirty.

"I thought you had gotten lost and then what would we have done?" Brandon asked in both a relieved and complaining manner.

"I was looking at some outfits and the time just flew by. Have you been waiting long?"

"Half-an-hour. That's O.K. Are you through with shopping? We need to get ready for the luau soon."

"What time does that start?"

"Six."

"We have plenty of time. Come on, let me show you the store I was last in. I want you to see some of these outfits for men. You haven't bought new clothes in ages." She grabbed his hand and they walked off together. Rose continued clinging to Brandon's hand on the sidewalk and he felt a sense of excitement coming from his wife that had been missing all day. Was she really excited or faking it, was the question Brandon carried with him for the next five blocks until they arrived at a store that totally disinterested him.

The luau was wonderful, as the dancers were delightful and the food scrumptious. It was the perfect environment. But Rose and Brandon hardly said a word to each other, as if they were strangers on a blind date that didn't turn out well. The couple enjoyed the other two couples at their table far more than each other. One couple was from Detroit, Michigan, elderly, full of laughs and jokes, and had been together for over forty years. They talked about their grandchildren, the pride of their lives. The other couple was from Lake Tahoe, California, and much younger. The husband was in the same line of work Brandon was doing, so both men had a common ground of conversation that could have lasted for hours. They also had four children, so the wife talked with Rose about the plusses and minuses of childrearing, with both agreeing that the benefits outweighed the liabilities.

Brandon, in the course of the two hours at the luau, was able to pinpoint one of the problems he had with Rose. He needed to stop comparing his enjoyment with her with what it was ten years ago when they were in Hawaii and, from what he could remember, at the same kind of luau in the same exact place. If he were to assess his enjoyment with Rose this evening it would come in as an average grade—not too bad, except that it was an "excellent" ten years ago. But why couldn't he just live in the here and now? He should act as if he were dating Rose for the first time. But instead, his memory would creep in as to what his erotic feelings for her used to be like, and those memories of the past dampened the present. Did Rose have the same problem with him? Probably, but it would be a good question to ask at breakfast the next morning. Rose was always more open to talking about their relationship than he.

They left the luau stuffed, and traded addresses with the delightful two couples that were sitting with them. It was after eight, and Brandon wanted to get home quickly to plan his strategy over the remainder of the evening.

5

They were in their hotel that evening at nine o'clock.

"I need to go out and get a drink, babe," Brandon said assertively.

"At this hour?"

"Yes, at this hour." He paused, then said, "After Brandy's lecture to both of us yesterday, I need to do some thinking at a bar and reflect what I'm going to say to her when we meet later in the week."

"She didn't lecture. She's just concerned."

"She lectured."

"Well, can't you do your thinking here?"

"I'd much rather go out for awhile. I did have a good time with you tonight. Really, I did. The food was great. And the people we were with were amusing."

"Yes, especially the elderly couple. That man was making a joke on just about every sentence. Well . . . if you must."

"You look tired. Maybe you should just go to bed. Or put your feet up and take a hot bath."

Brandon was over at Cassie's by nine-thirty. He had called her from a pay phone a few minutes earlier. He knocked on the door and heard a young feminine voice say, "I'll get it." Who could that be?

An attractive busty young blonde answered the door.

"Is this Cassie's place?"

"Yes, come on in," said the young girl vivaciously, eyeing Brandon from head to toe.

"Hello Brandon," said Cassie in the background. "Sarah, this is my old boyfriend from way back." Sarah put out her hand to Brandon and he gave it a gentle shake. It was the same touch that Cassie had. He didn't know whether this was a young roommate of Cassie's or her daughter.

"Brandon, this is my son Trevor." Cassie pointed to a man in his early twenties with a beard, lying back in a chair with his feet up reading a newspaper. He waved.

"And this is . . . Sarah, did you say?" Brandon asked, motioning to Sarah.

"Yes, my daughter."

"I knew about your son, but didn't know about your daughter."

"They're a year apart. Have a seat. Do you want something to drink? We have beer, wine, ginger ale, coke, milk, coffee."

"Ah, let me have a beer."

"We have Michelob, Bud. . . ."

"Any beer is fine."

Brandon noticed Sarah smiling at him as she leaned back into the edge of the couch opposite the end where Brandon was sitting. Well, let's see. He knew that her son was twenty-one, so that would make Sarah a ripe and mature twenty. Was she Trevor's full-blooded sister, or half-sister? That question could wait. Cassie went into the kitchen. Sarah took out a cigarette and lit it.

"So, are you in school?" Brandon asked Sarah.

"Journalism. I'm going only part-time. Night classes. I work during the day in a flower shop."

"In the city?"

"You mean Honolulu? Yes. On Wilder Avenue near Makiki. Work thirty-seven hours a week. My lunch break is from twelve to one." She blew out some smoke.

Good God, thought Brandon, why is she mentioning about her lunch break to me! Already, after only about twenty seconds of dialogue. She has been well-trained by somebody.

"I love the creative arts," she said. "But I'm taking my time with school while making some good money at the shop."

It was easy for Brandon to figure out his attraction to this young lady. Her features and mannerisms were very similar to Cassie's two decades ago, and Brandon felt he was in a time warp. For a few seconds, Cassie had slipped his mind. But then she came in with the drinks.

"There you are." Cassie handed him his glass of Michelob, while she and Sarah had wine. "Who cares about the drinking age?" Cassie snickered.

Cassie sat down in the middle of the couch, between Sarah and Brandon. Sarah's face showed a slight disappointment, but then winked her eye at Brandon when Cassie turned toward him.

"So do you have business meetings this week?" Cassie asked.

"Yes. On Wednesday and Thursday. For now."

"Brandon's involved with an advertising agency," Cassie turned to tell Sarah. "He's a big shot. Gets all of these fringe benefits with travel."

"No, I'm not a big shot. I'm not an account executive, but in accounting. I'm going to be showing some of our new software to a couple of clients is all. I'll be talking to their account group on how we will be using it."

"Sounds interesting," Sarah said.

"It's new up-to-date software showing how we can better project the rating points and shares of stations that will be advertising the products of these clients." Brandon thought how he hated to continue lying.

"And you've been here since . . . Saturday?" Cassie asked.

"Yes. I'm taking a couple of vacation days, Monday and Tuesday, and the rest of the week is designated a business trip starting Wednesday. But the company is paying for the roundtrip airfare."

"And how is . . . is it Rose? The divorce is final?"

Brandon paused. "Yes, it's final. As of two months ago. But we're still friends. The kids are taking it well . . . or as best as can be considered under the circumstances." He hated lying even more.

"How old are your kids?" asked Sarah.

"Nineteen, seventeen, fifteen, and . . . thirteen, I believe."

"You kept your wife busy," said Sarah. "Four kids . . . whew! Mom has her hands full with just two."

"Yes, and each of you two with your activities are equivalent to three kids each," Cassie scoffed.

"I don't cause you any trouble," Sarah reported.

"Oh please," Cassie replied, rolling her eyes.

Brandon continued to scan Cassie. He couldn't get himself excited over her. Not yet. Sarah was no problem. She was an absolute knockout, and was watching his every move and nuance, dissecting his every word.

"And where are you staying?" Cassie asked as she reached out and touched the top of his hand.

Brandon told her the name of the hotel instinctively. He then realized he should have lied about that as well, but couldn't take the words back.

They continued talking, while Sarah went through two more cigarettes and chimed in some jargon whenever she thought it appropriate. Cassie continued to touch Brandon's hand, rubbing it sensuously, and talking to him with her eyes focused squarely on his.

"Call me for lunch when you have the time, although I can't tomorrow, and we'll get together again," she said excitedly. "It was so good to see you, Brandon. You haven't lost your quiet charm." She hugged him, and he folded his arms around her and kissed her cheek when she was ready to kiss on the lips.

"I know you have work tomorrow," he said. He looked at his watch. "My word, it's ten-thirty already."

"What will you be doing tomorrow?" Cassie inquired. "Your business stuff isn't until Wednesday."

"Spending time on the beach, maybe go out to see Pearl Harbor. Drive out to see Waimea Falls, perhaps. Sightsee." Sarah had an intent gaze on him as she stood behind her mother a few feet.

"Give me a call," Cassie said smiling. "Please."

"Of course I will." He hugged her again. Sarah approached. "And nice to meet you, Sarah." He extended his arm, and she gave him a very strong hug instead.

"I guess Trevor has gone to bed," he said, trying to change the subject of Sarah's embrace in front of Cassie. Trevor appeared like a non-person at this meeting, and barked only twice.

"He keeps to himself, usually," Cassie explained. "He was extra tired tonight."

Brandon was in the front doorway when he reflected on how Sarah had kept her spotlight on him during the entire time. Brandon could not recall her looking anywhere else from the time he stepped in the door, and after saying goodbye he had a strong erection going back to his car.

He got back to his hotel at eleven. Rose was asleep, and it relieved him greatly to not have to lie about what bar he entertained. Her body was still on Pacific Standard Time at two in the morning. But when he got into bed, she rustled, then moved over and put her arms around him, before going to sleep again. Brandon stared at the ceiling for what seemed to be an hour.

6

The next day, Brandon was able to get to Sarah's flower shop in the late morning when he told Rose he was going to buy a small camera in the camera shop he saw yesterday. But he only had a few minutes.

Sarah was glad to see him. "Are you here to buy me a flower?" she asked.

"No, as a matter of fact."

She looked disappointed.

"Well, why not," he said. He took a rose from one of the larger vases, put it in a smaller vase and handed it to her. "There you are, my love." He paid the cashier.

"You only needed a little prompting," she said. "Thank you."

"I was going to the camera shop just a few blocks from here, so I thought I would see where you worked. Surprised?"

"Surprised."

"You've been working here how long?"

"Over a year. Brandon, are you still attracted to my mother?"

"What a question!"

"Why?" she snickered. "It's a good question, I think."

"Well . . . of course, she's aged somewhat. And I'm not any younger."

"And . . . so?"

"You are inquisitive. I don't need to answer."

"May I help you?" Sarah asked a customer.

"Where are your orchids? Do you have them?" the man customer asked.

"I can help you," she told him, and motioned for him to follow her.

She came back in a couple of minutes to where Brandon was standing.

"I have my lunch time in about half-an-hour," she told Brandon, rubbing shoulders with him.

"I don't have the time now, I'm sorry," said Brandon who was very sorry to say it. "I need to be somewhere. Tomorrow?"

"Tomorrow I will be spending my lunch hour at home. We could meet there?"

"Sure," said Brandon instinctively. He remembered that he was to be on a plane to Kauai tomorrow with Rose, but thought it didn't leave until two. The plane tickets were at the hotel, so he presently couldn't check them to make sure. "Yes, that will be good. Can I get the phone number here in case something comes up?"

She told him the number as he wrote it down on a receipt he had in his wallet.

"My business meeting tomorrow should be over by eleven," Brandon said. "If you don't hear from me," Brandon said, "then I will see you around . . . twelve- fifteen tomorrow at your place?"

"Perfect," she said with a beaming smile.

"I want to ask you some things about your mother and about yourself as well. Now stay out of trouble until I arrive."

"Not a chance."

He clasped her hand, then left. He went to the camera shop and bought a small camera so that Rose wouldn't get suspicious about his whereabouts.

"This is a portable camera I can carry in my pocket for tomorrow's trip to Kauai," he told Rose when he returned to her.

"We can share it, I hope. You tend to jiggle when you hit the click button."

"Come on, Rose, I'm not that bad at picture-taking," whined Brandon.

"With waterfalls and canyons, you're fine," Rose assured him. "With people, you tend to guillotine them. The pictures of people you take show them from the neck down."

"I'm not planning on taking pictures of people. Just nature."

"We're safe."

"I was thinking about you all last night," he said.

"No you weren't. I'm sure you slept," she said.

"Not much."

"That makes me nervous. Because, I don't know how this can work."

"You mean, because of your hubby?" he asked.

"Yes. Because of my charming, unexciting, dull hubby," she responded.

"Are you going to continue staying with him when you're unhappy?" he asked.

"I'm not totally unhappy. We have our moments," she answered.

"How often?" he asked.

"I don't have a stop-watch," was the only answer she could think of.

"Well, then it's your decision," he said assertively. "I can't make it for you. I only know I'm very happy when I'm with you, which has been only twice this week."

"And when I leave on Saturday, time will heal, won't it? You'll be fine," she said assuredly.

"No, it won't be that fine." Then he paused and said, "Don't you enjoy my company?"

"What a question. I *love* very much being in your company," she said passionately.

This dialogue was between Rose and Stan at four o'clock on the same day Brandon saw Sarah at the flower shop. They were conversing at a small diner in Honolulu. Rose met Stan ten years ago when she and Brandon visited Hawaii. Stan was working at the same advertising agency as Brandon, but Stan was in the Hawaii office, Brandon in the Los Angeles office. Stan and his wife at the time, Louise, went with Rose and Brandon on a helicopter ride in Kauai and also did some hiking. After Stan and Louise divorced, Rose looked him up last year when she and Brandon came to Hawaii to visit Brandy. They met twice then, unbeknownst to Brandon. They occasionally communicated by telephone in the weeks prior to this year's trip. When Brandon went off "shopping" yesterday, Rose took the opportunity to see Stan at his office on the ninth floor of a building that housed the agency. They talked incessantly to the point that Rose was late in meeting up with Brandon at a street corner.

The dialogue at the cafe continued:

"So what is Brandon doing right now, do you think?" Stan asked.

"Probably sitting out on the balcony," Rose said thoughtfully. "Drinking coffee, reading a magazine, or else watching baseball on T.V. lying back in bed."

"Do you still love him?"

"Oh Stan."

"Please."

"Our love is cold. Right now it is. That was the whole purpose of the trip. It's what our counselor wanted, to light a fire under us. To spark the love that has been burning out for years. Do I love him? No, I guess I don't right now. I still have a fantasy that we will love each other the way we used to, but we've been trying for years. There's a point when a couple begins to give up." She paused, and then began again: "And, I do like you Stan. I'm obviously trying to find something in you that isn't in my marriage. I need that *something*. But, you can't let Brandon know about this. You can't. He is still being faithful to me as far as I can tell. There's no reason for me to believe otherwise. And, if you want, you can continue to call me on the phone weekly at home during the day, even though it's expensive. I can't call you— it will come out on our phone bill."

Stan grabbed her hands in his. "I'm captivated by you, Rose. Know that." Then he sighed. He started to say something else, and then stopped. They were both silent for a long while.

Rose broke the silence in a rather uncanny way. "I need to use the restroom." She got up and started walking.

"I need to get rid of some coffee," replied Stan, following her.

They both came out of each restroom at the same time. Stan did not lose the opportunity, especially since they were in a hallway with no one around. He grabbed her around the shoulders, kissed her passionately, and when there was no resistance from her, kissed her again and again. When steps were heard, he stopped, and Rose was breathing hard and continued looking up into his eyes. He took her hand and escorted her back to their booth.

When they sat down, Rose said she had to go.

"Now?"

"Yes. I told Brandon I would be back at a certain time, and the hotel is about ten blocks away. I need to start walking now. And . . . we really can't be seen together, out there."

"I understand. So, when next?"

"I don't know. I hope to see you again, but I don't know when. I'm flustered." She rubbed her face.

"So am I."

Brandon checked the airline tickets to Kauai when he got home, and to his delight the plane would not leave until two just as he had remembered. It would give him plenty of time to see Sarah tomorrow. Thinking about Sarah and the chance to be with her made him feel twenty years younger.

He took Rose to dinner that night and it was at a place with an ocean view. He had two glasses of champagne, Rose had one. The champagne seemed to affect him more than usual. His mind went into a strange mode. Interesting possibilities plunged into his head. Why did marriage need to be a *lifelong* commitment? Why couldn't it be a ten year commitment and then a person was free? Or the couple could decide every ten years whether they wanted to stay together. If they decided to stay together, they would need to wait another ten years before deciding again. If they decided to part, they wouldn't need to mess with a divorce and all the legal stuff. They would just disband and be free. Or how about the seven-year plan? Every seventh year of the marriage they would be free to date or have a relationship with anyone else they chose—sort of like a year of liberation. At the end of that seventh year, the couple would decide if they would continue the marriage. If it continued, the seven-year cycle would start all over again. And you could only break it off with your spouse after every seven years. Then Brandon realized he had had way too much to drink. He would lay off the champagne for good while he was on his vacation. He thought of his parents and was glad they would never know his most recent thoughts. They had been a devoted couple to each other, married for forty-five years until his dad passed away.

His mother was currently in a rest home. They would both be embarrassed of his thoughts if they knew them. He really believed he was making a lifelong commitment to Rose on their wedding day. And she has been so faithful to him. He turned and looked at her with the ocean in the background. Even without the ocean she was still beautiful to him. Why could he not get *excited* about her anymore?

They got back to the hotel a very tired couple, still not adjusted to the three hour time difference from California. They tried lovemaking that evening which started good and ended badly, continuing a habit they couldn't seem to break.

7

Brandon arrived at Sarah's home at twelve-fifteen the next day, Wednesday, a couple of minutes after she had arrived from work. The day was clear and very warm, and her blonde hair glistened in the sun while she was waiting in the front lawn for him to arrive. She waved at him as his car approached. She was full of energy and excitement.

He knew she had to be back to her work by one so he needed to make quick work of this package of dynamite. He walked quickly up to her like a schoolboy.

"Let's go inside," she said, grabbing his hand.

Inside, she turned on the air conditioner and then plopped herself down on the living room couch. Brandon sat next to her.

"I have some questions. Just out of curiosity, you know," he said.

"Shoot."

"I don't think I got the whole story regarding your mother, and everything that happened some twenty years ago. She was married at the time she had Trevor, correct?"

"She had been married for three months when he was born," Sarah said very directly.

"And I take it she married the real father of Trevor?"

"Yes she did."

"And, are you Trevor's full-blooded sister, or half-sister?"

"Half-sister. She's my real mom, and my dad . . . well . . . he. . . ."

"You don't have to talk about it if you don't want, Sarah. I'm just curious."

"Oh, I know that. I appreciate that you want to know about me, because that shows you really care. Of course you want to know my background, and that flatters me." She came over and sat on his lap. Brandon was embarrassed for a split second, but it felt so good where she was located that all embarrassment vanished. She then put her arms around his neck. Brandon felt her luscious bottom right over his genitals and forgot the subject they were talking about. "She met my real father in a night club. It was a one-night stand. They had sex at his apartment. She got pregnant, and couldn't believe it. She had to tell Ron—Ron was Trevor's dad, she was still married to him at the time. The marriage was a disaster from the start and she was lonely in it, even the first year. She married Ron because, well, she was carrying his child and thought it was the best thing to do. She told him about me because he would have eventually figured out that I wasn't his child. My real dad's features were nothing like his. So my mom told him up front, which was a good thing. Ron tried to get my mom to do away with me because I wasn't born yet. She told him she would never do such a thing. She didn't believe in that. So anyway, they divorced. It wasn't only because of me, though. They would have divorced eventually anyway. That's what my mom always told me. He was not a good man. A hard worker at his job, responsible. But he was not a good man, morally. I'm very grateful my mom had me. We've been good for each other, regardless of what we may say about each other when there's company around." She gave a little laugh. "Really, we have been good for each other. She made the right choice, and also the right choice to let the divorce go through. She would have been miserable with him."

Brandon tenderly squeezed her posterior and she turned and looked him straight in the eyes very closely. She waited for him to make another move, and when he didn't, she kissed him very sensuously on the lips. Then they kissed each other again and again.

"You are a beautiful girl, Sarah. And you're mature for your age."

"Why? How do you know how old I am?"

"Simple mathematics. You act like a woman in her late twenties, but you are . . . only twenty?

"That's right."

"Whatever happened to your father?"

"He's around still. He has a family of his own now, happily married with kids."

"But do you ever see him?"

"I used to see him about every other weekend when I was a little girl. My mom and he stayed good acquaintances. Not close friends, just good acquaintances. Then when he got married and had other kids of his own, I kind of faded from the picture. He stays in touch occasionally."

"Hmm," was all Brandon could say. He was in seventh heaven with this blonde doll.

"So, now about yourself. You mentioned the other night you have four kids. Teenagers."

"Four kids. Two girls, two boys." Brandon stopped short of mentioning his oldest was here in Hawaii and at the University. He wouldn't want Sarah to look her up. He quickly changed the subject. "And I'm working at an advertising agency in the accounting department. Been there for about twelve years now. We have another office here in Hawaii and that is why I am over here—on business."

He didn't know whether Sarah was really listening to his last sentences. She kissed him fervently, and then surveyed his eyes and the features of his face.

"What are your kids' names again?"

"Brandy, Jana, Lester, James."

"Cute names. The oldest is Brandy?"

Brandon nodded. "We thought our first was going to be a boy and we were to call him Brandon Jr., so we made a little adjustment."

"When was the last time you had a girl sit on your lap like this?" she asked.

Brandon smiled and gave a little chuckle. "Long time ago."

Cassie immediately walked in the front door.

Everyone froze. Cassie didn't bother closing the door, and took her time staring at Sarah first, then Brandon.

After a deathly silence, Sarah said to her mother, "Brandon has been telling me a lunchtime story."

"Ah, yes I have," said Brandon. "She's right . . . absolutely."

Cassie shut the front door.

"You know mother, I didn't hear you come up the driveway for some reason or another. And why are you home now? You never come home during lunch." Sarah found a way to stay calm, remaining on Brandon's lap and her hands clasped around his neck.

"Well, actually," Cassie started. "Actually I came home from the bank so I could make an extended phone call to you, Brandon, in case you were at your hotel. I didn't want to use the bank phones."

"Well, what a coincidence," said Brandon. "Well, here I am. You can talk to me now if you wish."

"Mother *never* comes home during her lunch hour," Sarah said confidingly to Brandon in a whisper close to his ear. Brandon took Sarah's hands from his neck and put them down in Sarah's lap. "Sarah, I think it is time to get off my lap now."

"Is the story over?" Cassie asked, looking as if she were going to faint.

"It is now, yes," said Brandon.

"Sarah, don't you need to get back to the flower shop by one?" her mother asked.

"Oh, I have plenty of time to get back," she replied, getting up from Brandon's lap.

"I think you better get back *before* one," Cassie said. "God, I feel faint." She put her hand on her forehead. "I really do." Cassie walked toward the kitchen. Brandon got up.

"Don't get up Brandon," Cassie said. "I'll be all right." She went in the kitchen.

Sarah gave Brandon a quick kiss. "I got to go." Then she whispered, "I'll talk to you later, I promise." Sarah walked out the front door.

Brandon followed her out the door. Sarah drove out of the driveway and waved to Brandon. Before Brandon could reach his car door, Cassie came outside.

"Brandon. We will need to talk about this."

Brandon got in his car. "Yes, at some point, I guess." He turned on the ignition with Cassie standing with her arms folded about six feet away. Off the cuff, he said, "You're beautiful. And you have a beautiful daughter." He drove off.

Brandon got back to the hotel a few minutes after one, and expected Rose to be there because of the flight leaving at two. But she was not in the room. Where could she be?

As the minutes ticked away, he was somewhat nervous about the flight, but not as much as he expected. The shocking appearance of Cassie a few minutes before was still in his system to the point that everything else almost deflected off of him and had no effect.

Rose arrived at one-thirty, running into the room.

"Oh, I'm sorry, Brandon."

"Goodness, where were you?"

"Busy with shopping, and I lost track of the time." She looked into the closet and got the extra clothes she needed. "I'll be ready in two minutes. I promise."

"Well, the flight leaves at two. It will take fifteen minutes to get to the airport. Remember, we're not spending the night in Kauai, so don't bring too much."

"It's sight-seeing, and then the luau tonight, right? You have the tickets for that?"

Brandon checked his wallet. He had the plane tickets and the luau tickets. "All here."

They left hurriedly, and arrived at the small airport ten minutes before take-off. The small luggage they had could be taken with them on board, and the person taking their tickets was calm, saying they had plenty of time. Brandon had to keep reminding himself it was not like the L.A. International Airport. They got on a small plane that would take about forty passengers.

The flight from Oahu to Kauai was so quick that Brandon had wished it were longer. Rose barely had the time to tell Brandon all of the shopping she had done, what she saw and what she bought.

The last time the two saw Kauai was ten years ago with Stan and Louise.

When they were landing, Rose reflected out loud, "I wonder what has happened with Stan and Louise. You remember? Stan used to work for your company."

"I remember. Stan quit the company years ago. They divorced, and that was a tragedy. They were such a fun couple." They landed in the city of Lihue, rented a car, and went to see Wailua Falls, Spouting Horn, Waimea Canyon, and the

Kalalau Lookout. Brandon used his new little camera often, and the couple went from place to place faster than could be imagined. Brandon had the trip mapped out, and they were able to arrive at the Luau only a few minutes late.

Brandon and Rose were equally quiet toward each other during the afternoon and evening—quiet even for them. They were thinking, in the back of their minds, about the course of events which happened to each of them during the lunch hour. But they were able to thoroughly enjoy nature and the beautiful scenery that was given to them as if it were gift-wrapped. They took a plane back to Oahu at nine-thirty on a special late flight.

Back at the hotel the same evening, Brandon immediately went into the restroom. He thought he was hearing things when he heard Sarah's voice in the next room. He listened more closely and realized it was a message Sarah left on the recording of their phone. A blaze of panic engulfed Brandon, as he knew Rose was listening to it attentively. He could hear Sarah talking about future plans with him and her apology of how things turned out during the lunch hour. Brandon did not have much time to think of a mode of attack. Damn these modern hotels with their new modern devices like these answering machines in the rooms. He remembered on Monday night telling Cassie and Sarah the specific hotel he was staying at, and could kick himself for forgetting to tell them not to contact him at the hotel. He also remembered Cassie mentioning at her house today that she was intending to call him, but his mind was in such a shock he also forgot to tell her not to contact him. What was Rose thinking right now? He contemplated for a few seconds, and then exited the restroom to face the music.

"Who was that on the recording?" he asked.

"A girl named Sarah," Rose said blandly.

"Sarah who?"

"You know who."

"What do you mean, I know who? I don't know a Sarah."

"Well, she apparently knows you very well."

"Let me hear the recording again."

Rose pushed the button. Sarah greeted Brandon, and talked about seeing him again as she qualified for a discount of a couple of airline tickets to Maui, and when could he go? She apologized if it was uncomfortable for Brandon when her mother came home, but it felt so good to be touched and kissed by him. She told him to call at her work. Brandon shook his head while the recording was going on.

"She obviously has the wrong Brandon. I'm sure there is another Brandon in this hotel, and the hotel operator gave her the wrong one."

"Shall I go down to the front desk, and see if there is more than one Brandon?" Rose said, not even suspiciously, but sarcastically.

He didn't answer, but Rose appeared to be leaving the room.

"You mean to tell me, Rose Lee Peeters, that at eleven o'clock at night you are actually going to go down and bother the front desk people as to whether there is more than one Brandon in this hotel?"

"That's what they are there for, to handle problems," she said.

"You don't trust me?"

"No. Not really."

Rose came back to the room after fifteen minutes.

"There is only one person with the name of Brandon registered in the hotel," she said.

He was already in bed with his back turned to her, trying to sleep. He had already pulled a calf muscle when stretching. "That's nice," he said, in response to Rose's statement.

Rose sighed. She took her time undressing for a few minutes, and then got into bed. Brandon kept his back to her and couldn't sleep, but tried to pretend he was. He was motionless for a half hour and then wanted to get up and go to the restroom but was worried he would be confronted with Rose again. He stayed motionless and couldn't hear Rose next to him. Was she O.K.? He finally rustled in bed but didn't turn around to look at her. He thought of going outside and getting some fresh air, but Rose would be suspicious. Finally an air of exhaustion crept into him, and, after what seemed to be an eternity, he finally dozed off.

8

Rose and Brandy were lying out on the beach at Waikiki the next day around noon.

"So he continued denying it this morning?" asked Brandy.

"Yeah, he wouldn't owe up to it. We were able to have breakfast together and I brought up the subject once. He said he didn't know her and went off to another subject. That was that. We had nothing scheduled for today, and both of us weren't saying much to each other, so we went our separate ways."

"I'm glad you called, mom. Although this has been very stressful to me, I can't see you two splitting up. But now you just gave me an example of what he did—or what you think he did—and I, I don't know what to do."

"Do nothing," said Rose, putting her hand on Brandy's cheek, and then withdrawing it. "It's not your worry. You can't do anything. It's like watching someone die of cancer. It is beyond your control. All one can do is hope, pray, or light candles, or something. But a person can't really do anything within their own power. They need to resort to some outside power. At this point, you must stay as emotionally uninvolved as you can."

"That's impossible. I love you two very much."

"I know. And I called you because . . . well, I needed to unload on somebody and you were the only one around. I didn't want to tell you this to put a burden on you."

"But maybe he really *doesn't* know this woman, this girl. Are you sure?"

"I'm sure. A woman always knows."

"What did you say her name was? Sally?"

"No. It doesn't matter what her name is."

Brandy turned over on her stomach and put her face in the beach blanket for a few seconds, then turned to her mother again and was about to say something, then stopped.

Rose immediately thought about Stan, and admitted silently to herself the mental unfaithfulness to both her husband and daughter. She knew it wasn't fair to talk about Brandon's indiscretions without talking about her own with Stan. But she still refrained in divulging this to Brandy, and would deal with her guilt at a later time. She looked out at the ocean and saw the tall waves crash against the shore, the cumulus clouds in the blue sky as a backdrop to the seagulls and doves, and realized that she had never seen anything so beautiful.

"If you divorce, are you going to bring up adultery as your reason?" was the ugly sentence from Brandy that interrupted Rose's view of breathtaking beauty.

"I have not thought that far yet. I know that if it is broken off, that I can probably find something in another man that I have been missing with Brandon over the last few years." There, she thought. She has thrown out the fleece. Let's see what Brandy does with it.

Brandy was hesitant, and then said, "I can't even *imagine* you with another man. Not even *imagine*. I've always known you as my mother, and as someone married to my dad. To see you even having lunch with another man and having a romantic flair is beyond my comprehension. I don't think I could handle it."

"Don't say anything more," Rose said quickly. She had her inquisition answered. "Have you ever gone snorkeling?"

"Yes, twice. And do you have a certain man in mind?"

"No." Rose turned on her side, so she could look more directly into Brandy's face. "I would like to go snorkeling. I've never gone and always wanted to try."

"Oh mother. You'd probably get scared and wouldn't be able to pull it off."

Rose immediately lost her interest. "Mm, well then, you are probably right. Maybe the next time we visit Hawaii."

"Are you two planning to come back again?"

"I don't know why I said that." She turned to lie on her back again. "So . . . are you still seeing Ron?"

"Haven't seen him in six months. I told you we broke it off. I told you on the telephone months ago."

"That's right. I forgot. You met him at the University, didn't you? He was also into journalism."

"No, he was studying to be a P.E. teacher. He should graduate this year. I wanted someone that would be committed to me. He didn't want any commitment. He probably had other girls he was seeing."

After Brandon had breakfast with Rose that morning, he waited for her to leave for the beach before going to a pay phone to call both Cassie and Sarah at their respective places of work to not call him at the hotel. He left his message with a co-worker of Cassie's at the bank, because he didn't want a dialogue with her. He was able to talk to Sarah directly.

"Well, now let's see," Sarah surmised out loud to Brandon. "Who could possibly hear my messages in your room? The maid? A butler? The errand boy? Or someone more exciting, like . . . a hula dancer you just picked up that is spending the night?"

"Seriously, dear Sarah, do *not* call my room. It's not. . . ."

"But how will I be able to contact you, lover? I may need you tonight."

What a nymph, a siren resurrected from the Odyssey, and where has this beautiful damsel been all my life? Brandon was already aroused by her voice alone.

"Do *not* call me at the hotel, or if you do I definitely won't see you again."

"Well, I'm sure a handsome middle-aged man like you certainly has a girlfriend floating around somewhere on this island and you don't want to be interrupted at the hotel, is that it?"

"No. No, that's not it. Look it, I have your work phone number. In the late afternoon sometime I can call you as to where we can hang out, O.K.? Is that a plan?"

"You leave when? Saturday? This is already Thursday. You'd better make it fast."

"I could call at about five-thirty when your shop closes. Then we can meet together somewhere and drive off to a faraway restaurant miles from here."

"You're not still married are you?"

"Sarah, did you just hear what I told you?"

"Yes I did."

"I got to go, and so do you." Brandon put in some more money in the phone. There was some silence, and then he said, "Are you still there?"

"Yes I'm still here, babe."

"The marriage for all practical purposes was over years ago. Call you this afternoon if I can."

"I don't know why you're worried about mom. She can't call the police on you. I'm an adult."

"I know you're an adult."

"She adores you. She's mad and a little disgusted with you as well, but there's nothing she can really do."

"Did she lecture you about yesterday?"

"Of course she did," Sarah said, and then started giggling. "For about fifteen minutes . . . a solid lecture that I am to stay away from you, and to not tempt middle-aged men who would love to take advantage of young girls any chance they get."

"I'm not trying to take advantage of you. Believe me. I just need some serious romance in my life again, and you brought a youthful cool wind back into my soul. I can't explain it. You wouldn't understand."

"I'm extremely bright. Don't treat me like I'm a naive little girl. I may be naughty at times, but I have an intelligent mind. I'm not impulsive either. I analyze things well, and then set my course of action, you know?"

The operator wanted some more money.

"O.K. got to go, sweetie. I don't have any change left. Be good, and I'll catch you later." He hung up.

Brandon went back to the hotel and turned on some baseball. The game was at Wrigley Field, Chicago, in a time zone that was five hours later. He made some coffee for himself, and lay back in his easy chair putting his feet up. He watched some of the game while also reading a novel. He thought of Sarah, and didn't care that he was about twice her age and old enough to be her father. The fact the world contained many other women just like Sarah on other islands and continents gave him exuberant joy. For the first time he could remember, there was *completely* no desire to stay married to Rose. The inkling of hope was now totally vanished. He looked forward to the rest of the day, especially the evening, and decided to relax and see where it would go and where it would lead him. Life has more to offer if we just give it a chance. Where was Rose at this moment? He didn't know, and didn't care.

Rose went snorkeling with Brandy that afternoon, and actually enjoyed it. Brandy remained reserved and non-talkative. Rose did not want to go back to the hotel to see Brandon that afternoon so after the snorkeling the two of them went shopping. Rose was somewhat surprised at how morose Brandy was during the hours with her. It was frightening. She could not remember her ever acting this way, and the depression she conveyed left an unpleasant aura around their companionship. It was to the point that Rose did not want to leave her alone when they were ready to depart at six that evening.

"I'm fine, mother. You need to go back to the hotel and see father."

"If he's there."

"I'm tired. I need to rest."

"You look so depressed."

"I'm just tired. Very tired. The snorkeling, the sun, shopping. I'm just worn out." She looked away from her mother, apparently to hide tears.

Rose gave her a big hug. "I know you're not happy about me and your dad. Get some rest. I love you."

Brandy turned around to face her mother. "Take care of yourself," she said, then walked away back to her car.

9

Brandon fell asleep towards the end of the Cubs game with a newspaper in his lap. When he awoke it was mid-afternoon. He remembered that being close to the ocean would often make him more relaxed and drowsy.

Rose had not returned. He would fix himself some lunch and coffee. If she didn't return to the hotel in an hour he was going to leave. That way he wouldn't need to make an excuse to her as to why he left.

He stuffed himself with two sandwiches, some fruit, and some pie and ice cream from the fridge. He felt disappointment when he heard rustling outside the front door and thought for sure it was Rose. But it was the maid coming in to clean, and felt relieved. After some coffee, he wrote a note to Rose mentioning he waited for her to return from the beach, and when she didn't come back, he got bored and left to amuse himself and wouldn't be back until about ten that evening. He left the hotel at about three, carrying a jacket with him.

Brandon found a bar downtown with a television set. He ordered a beer and certain scenes crept into his mind from the past. Family scenes from long ago barged their way into his thoughts, even though he didn't want them in. It was as if a powerful force were telling him to observe something.

He remembered coming to his home in Whittier from a long day's work, walking through the front door and there was Rose who was waiting to greet him. She showed him her effervescent smile and flooded him with kisses.

"Daddy's home!"   Someone shouted in the background. It was five-year old Lester. Someone else could be heard dropping some toys at the news and little feet were pattering on the hardwood floor toward their father. It was seven-year old Jana. Brandy, nine, was closest to the front door and put down her Nancy Drew book and walked to her dad. Three-year-old James was crawling through the hallway pretending to be an elephant, and crawled faster to the front door. Brandy leaped up to give her dad a kiss on the cheek, and Jana leaped up into his arms and gave him a bear hug around the neck. Lester got as close to his father as he could, cuddled Brandon's leg and looked up at him with a respectful smile as he received some strokes of affection on the top of his head from dad. James grabbed his father's leg and started shaking it and yelling "Daddy, daddy, daddy, you're home!" Then, of course, there was the family dog, Sparks, who had to get into the action and excitement, running toward Brandon and barking, leaping around trying to find an opening between family members to get to his beloved master. The commotion had proven again that "dad" coming home from work was the highlight of the day for this household. Brandon staggered from the sheer weight of his children and had to carefully sit down in the entry way, but it didn't cause the excitement to subside. The children continued hugging and shaking, while Sparks was able to get his tongue to reach Brandon's face with affectionate licks from the forehead to the chin. The sound of screaming, laughing, and barking finally subsided after a couple of minutes. Then each family member would eventually leave very slowly, one by one, and go back to what they were doing, leaving Brandon almost breathless from the boundless affection given to him.

Brandon remembered another scene at Green Valley Lake up in the mountains where he would always take his family each summer. They loved to rent a cabin and enjoy the outdoors, including the swimming area that had been set aside for young families. He was teaching his youngest son James, who was six at the time, how to swim while the rest of the family was on the sandy beach finishing up eating their drumsticks. Although nervous, James was trying to learn his swimming strokes while kicking with his feet, as Brandon held his son's stomach to make sure he didn't go under. All of a sudden, Brandon was drenched with water from the pails of his other three children coming from behind. He was left totally defenseless, as the children continued to fill their pails with water and throw the moisture over their dad amidst howls of laughter. All he could do was take Lester in his arms and run out onto the sand only to be drenched again with pails of water. So dad went on offense. He grabbed each of the older kids and separately through them into the water amid their shrieks of delight.

Some quick flashes of shorter scenes were whipping through.   He remembered the campfires at night when they were camping and the close-knit family atmosphere of those days, the bedtime stories he would read to his children and the mutual kiss before they would go to sleep to end their day. He recalled, when Rose was sick, taking all four children to three different schools in the morning before he went to work in Los Angeles, and receiving a hug and kiss from each one of them, in their own separate style.

Brandon took another swig of beer and contemplated how things could have changed so drastically over the years. What happened? Did the kids start drifting apart from each other when he and Rose started drifting apart? Was it only mom and dad who changed toward each other, while the rest of the family stayed intact?   Would the other kids react the same way Brandy is reacting when they are told the news? Do they really know, yet, how unhappy their parents are about each other? They are still teenagers that are so sensitive, not the same way as a five-year-old, but still sensitive in their vulnerability. Brandon thought about what he should do regarding this situation, and then immediately threw it from him—he could not bear to think of it now. Brandon's longing for excitement was *too* enticing. His passion for good romance was *too* great. He was going to have a good time with a cute young lady this evening and felt he deserved it, especially with the way Rose had been putting her foot in his mouth every other time he opened it for the last two years. Life was to be enjoyed, and he was not going to let anyone mar it, or allow scenes from the past to get in his way.

1 0

Brandon stayed at the bar for a couple of hours, watched another baseball game on television there, and then went to a nearby restaurant for a snack. At five-thirty he called Sarah from a pay phone and they agreed to meet on a street corner within walking distance of where he was.

"Can we take my car?" he asked her when she arrived a few minutes after six.

"Of course. My car is parked only two blocks away and is safe."

"You look absolutely gorgeous. You did something with your hair. By the way, will your mom get suspicious?"

"No. I went straight home after you called. I told her I was getting a prescription downtown."

"But . . . wouldn't she expect you back soon?"

"Oh Brandon, listen," Sarah responded in a calm but aggressive tone, shifting her weight in the front seat as they drove off. "I'm an adult, not a child. Mom has to realize that. I don't report to her. I live in the same house she does. That's all. She lectured me again last night, and I just stared at her. I didn't really respond." Sarah put her arm around his and cuddled close to him, taking off her seatbelt. Brandon felt heavily aroused.

"Don't worry about my mom," she continued. "She's fine. I know you liked her at one time and you want to remain friends with her. At least she said you do. Let's enjoy the evening."

"We're driving to Waimanalo Beach Park. It's several miles from Honolulu, but there is a restaurant right on the coast. Do you mind?"

"Not at all," she said. "It will give me plenty of time to tell you about my goals in life, my studies at the University, and tell you about . . . just me."

"That will be the most interesting thing for me to hear," Brandon assured. "I just want to make sure we are plenty of miles away. I don't want anyone to apprehend me from my work. Not at this time. The Honolulu office where I am visiting on a business trip is large. I also do not want to be seen by anyone who knows Cassie and you. She has a lot of friends, I'm sure."

"I understand your thoughts," Sarah replied. "But eventually, if we're going to have a dating relationship, you can't be secretive. You should be willing to be seen with me in the middle of a crowd—whether it be Waikiki Beach or Times Square."

"And that will come about," Brandon said quickly. "Just . . . not now. I leave Oahu in about forty-eight hours. At this time, I just want to be *really* alone with you." He smiled passionately at her, taking his eyes off of the road. She smiled back, and then planted a long smooch on his lips. Brandon breathed heavily, putting one hand behind Sarah's head as if to make even stronger the force of her kiss, then returned his sight to his driving. Sarah continued looking erotically into his eyes, while Brandon thought intently about the fact he had not been kissed like that in years. She put her hands through his hair, stroking it consistently, as if she were taking the tempo from a metronome. "Thank you," he told her softly, in gratitude.

They arrived at Waimanalo State Park just before sunset and had a fish dinner at a restaurant overlooking the beach. After dinner, they walked out onto the beach clasping hands and saw the beautiful sunset that Brandon had dreamed all day he would see. Continuing to walk on the sand towards the water, they appreciated the high, silvery waves. Brandon turned Sarah towards himself, kissing and fondling her just as the sun went below the horizon. There was no one on the beach where they were, and each of them could feel the warm winds from the sea. Both felt they were in a different galaxy separate from the rest of humanity, and this special moment was placed in the eternity of time reserved only for them. Brandon felt the years of unfulfilled desires of intimacy and affection being fulfilled at this moment, and nothing could destroy this time of ecstasy for him. All of the money and time he had spent for this trip to Hawaii for the sake of himself and Rose had been worth it through the affectionate lovemaking of young Sarah.

He turned her body so that she was facing the ocean, while he was facing the land covered with houses and other buildings. He checked to make sure no one was in the vicinity, then unfastened her blouse and dropped it on the sand. Brandon then took off her bra and caressed her luscious breasts while continuing to kiss her.

"Oh mercy," she said, extremely aroused. Brandon's seductive touch enlarged her breasts even more. She was breathing very heavily and gave ecstatic groans of pleasure. Sarah began repeating his name, over and over, countless times as he continued to kiss and fondle her. He could feel her body temperature rising. Within minutes they were in darkness, the only light coming from the commercial buildings and a crescent moon.

Brandon knew she wanted full unbridled sex somewhere in a room, but he didn't know whether she was on the pill and he didn't bring any contraceptives. They continued kissing, and finally Brandon dropped down to the sand with fatigue.

"Are you all right? What's wrong?" she asked anxiously.

"Nothing's wrong. Everything is right. I haven't received this much in so long. I feel like a complete man again. You made me feel complete. It feels so good to be loved, to experience intimacy that is *real* and not done out of mere duty. You wouldn't understand."

"Of course I understand, my sweet," she said adoringly, rubbing his face. Sarah, ironically, acted very maternal, looking over Brandon who was crouched down, like a mother over her son who had just been healed with a band-aid. She put her fingers through his hair, looking adoringly in his eyes. Then, Sarah sat down in the sand with him.

"Do you like the sound of the ocean?" she asked, with no answer needed.

"Especially when you can't hear anything else," he replied. They didn't speak for awhile, but let nature communicate sounds to them.

Brandon lay down with his face looking up into the sky with the first stars of the evening beginning to appear. Sarah lay next to him, and rested her head below his left shoulder. "Heaven," he said.

They were silent for a few minutes. Then Sarah got up and kneeled over him saying, "Your former wife must not have given the intimacy you needed. I could tell. I could tell tonight, and . . . actually I could tell when you first visited us Monday night."

"Really?"

"Yes. I mean . . . you looked happy because you were seeing mom again for the first time in years. But you also had that forlorn look, as if you were saying, 'If I don't have a romantic fling, or a female doesn't caress my crotch real soon, I'm going to die on the spot.' It was a sad look, not really something that could be seen on the outside, but a sad countenance look."

Brandon nodded his head, and continuing to be amazed at the social maturity and astuteness of this young lady.

"Well, you have someone now," she said.

"I'm supposed to leave the island in two days."

"You will be back."

"How do you know?"

"Because I think you will. Or I will come see you. Where did you say you lived in California? You told me at dinner. Was it Upland?"

"That's right. I moved there from Whittier four years ago."

She lay back down with him for a few more minutes. They got up when it was after nine and began walking back to the car. Brandon put his arm around her beautiful figure, and she put her left hand in his hip pocket.

"Do you want to find a room?" she asked.

"No," he said immediately. He was very prepared to answer the question.

"Are you sure? And why not?"

"Are you on the pill?"

"No."

"It's not safe. I didn't bring anything, and . . . it would not be a good idea. I want to enjoy the rest of the evening on our first night out as much as I have already. And I know if I got a hotel room, I'd be there the whole night with you and wouldn't want to leave. I have a business meeting tomorrow, early, and need to be rested. And, as I said before, it wouldn't be safe for you. So it would be best. . . ."

"O.K., that's all right," Sarah interrupted. "That's fine. We can talk on the way back to Honolulu in the car. I'll be looking forward to that. I have plenty more to tell you."

Brandon was able to find a parking spot two blocks away from her car when they got back into Honolulu.

"I will call you tomorrow, I promise," he said. "At noon, or maybe twelve-thirty would be better."

"But when will I see you?"

"I don't know." He was going to mention about Rose, and then caught himself. That was a close one. He was tired, and all of the caressing and kissing had taken the stuffing out of him, hurting his thinking process. "I want to see you desperately. I . . . hope to see you tomorrow."

"I can't see you at your hotel?" she asked.

"I'll call you sometime after my business meeting, and we'll set up a place where we can meet. Like we did tonight." He looked at her and sighed and smiled at the same time. She smiled back. They kissed passionately.

"Thanks for a heavenly evening," she said.

"What are you going to tell your mother about getting the prescription?"

She laughed. "I told you not to worry about my mother, didn't I?" Sarah said, wagging her index finger at him. "I already got the prescription before I met you tonight. I'll tell her I went to a bar afterward, even though you have to be twenty-one to go in one, and I met someone a couple of years older. I had my Seven-up, he had his beer."

"Sounds like a plan, I guess."

They got out of his car and walked hand-in-hand to her car. She drove off after a final look, a final embrace, and a final kiss. He watched her drive off and remained motionless in the middle of the street about eight feet from the curb.

Brandon heard a car door slam behind him, turned, and saw Trevor, Sarah's half-brother, about forty feet away on the sidewalk. Trevor stared intently at Brandon and began approaching him. Brandon immediately smelled troubled, and instinctively began running away from Trevor toward his car parked two blocks away. He looked back and saw Trevor running toward him yelling obscenities. Brandon didn't know whether Trevor had a gun or knife, but panicked that his life was in danger. Could he outrun Trevor for two city blocks? After crossing a street he heard behind him a screech of brakes and a car horn, but didn't turn around to see if Trevor was still chasing him. He reached his car with the keys ready to unlock the door. Brandon got inside, locked the door, and started the ignition. Out of panic, he did not bother to check for oncoming traffic, but made it into the lane of traffic just as Trevor tried to open the car door on the driver's side. Trevor bounced off of the car, yelling more obscenities, and threats. Brandon drove off, taking a minute to catch his breath. He felt a tightening in his chest for a few seconds but then appeared all right when he began to breathe normally.

Brandon got to his hotel in ten minutes, parked his car, and then tried to evaluate everything. He believed Trevor would have killed him if he could. Perhaps Cassie got worried about her daughter being out so long and sent Trevor to the drug store where she was to get the prescription, to find her. Trevor apparently found Sarah's car near the drug store as she was leaving. Brandon didn't know whether Trevor was sober or drunk, but could feel the hatred from him for his involvement with his half-sister. The exuberant evening with Sarah and his release from formerly unfulfilled desires had been turned into a frantic, panic-stricken chase down a sidewalk. Brandon didn't know whether Trevor was still searching for him, but knew he had better get inside the building.

Brandon conjectured he would need to face Rose when he got to his room.   But he felt odds were two to one that Rose would be tamer than Trevor.

11

It was after six o'clock when Rose came back to the hotel room after spending most of the day with Brandy. She read Brandon's note about not returning until ten and had mixed emotions. There was the hope that perhaps she and Brandon would not go anywhere that evening but just sit and relax, and talk about anything that would be congenial. They needed to do better with their communication skills and this would be the opportunity to let their marriage counselor know that an effort was made. But Brandon would probably watch television and ignore her or do some thinking out on the porch by himself with his coffee. She wasn't going to agitate herself wondering where Brandon *really* was, because she knew it was with the woman who called on the telephone last night. Rose knew it as well as knowing she was in Hawaii. So it gave her a tinge of excitement that she was going to have the evening to herself—and she thought of having it with Stan.

Rose sat on the couch and thought deeply about her options, putting her head in her hands. Then she got up, picked up the phone, and started dialing, then put the phone down. She went downstairs and used a payphone to call Stan. He was excited to hear from her, and offered to pick her up. But Rose declined for fear of being apprehended, and told him she would get a taxi because Brandon had the car. He gave her directions to his condo about ten miles away.

Unlike her husband, Rose did not use any caution with her lover, spending ample time in bed with Stan at his condo, amidst two glasses of champagne and other alcohol.

"Are you sure you can get back to your hotel, O.K.?" asked Stan. He grinned, and then asked, "Can you even see straight?"

"I'm all right."

"Rose, why not just spend the night here. It may be unsafe for you to drive, and I'm going to worry over you."

"I took a cab to get here, remember? I'll take a cab back. And I need to be back by ten."

"Are you worried about your husband finding out? Are you crazy? You know he isn't being faithful to you either. I know you're suspicious of him too. He may be with someone else tonight."

"I don't want him to know anything, do you understand?" Rose said with agitation. Then she sat down on the sofa, putting her head in her hands. "Oh God, I've never cheated on him before," she said rather softly. "And I don't want him to know. It's been over twenty years of marriage and I don't want him to know." She got up and gathered her things.

"Rose, listen, I have an idea that might work," said Stan, trying to stop her from leaving. Rose headed for the door. Stan followed. She kissed him on the lips and left. Rose had already arranged for a cab to pick her up just a few minutes before ten.

When Brandon walked through the door, Rose was sitting on the couch reading magazines. She looked up at him and stared, then put down the magazine beside her.

"Did you have a good evening?" she asked.

"Yes. Saw the ocean. A sunset. Did a lot of driving. How 'bout yourself?"

"You know, we could have used this time tonight to communicate. I mean, *really* communicate. Work out problems. But the night is gone. What are we going to tell Tim?" she asked, referring to their counselor.

"Don't know. We don't have to report to him. He's not our boss, or our baby-sitter."

"He's trying to help us," Rose said. She stood up, and got close to Brandon and looked intently in his eyes. "You were with Sarah tonight. I know."

"And how do you know that?" he asked quickly.

"I just know," she said as she continued looking at him.

Brandon was caught in what he thought was a trap. His mental rolodex was rapidly turning with questions and options. Did Rose see them together when they drove off? Or when they came back? Perhaps Trevor contacted the hotel room and talked to Rose. He was listening to the conversation Monday night in Cassie's living room so he knew what hotel to call. Damn him. Regardless, the way Rose was looking at him he knew that she knew.

Rose continued looking at him. He turned and put his jacket in the closet and then returned to the place where he had been standing. Maybe she really didn't know for sure. Brandon was too tired to play games. If he lied about it, she would know for certain it was a lie if she saw them together. If she didn't have any proof, her eyes and the way she looked made it appear she did. Brandon sighed deeply, looked at her, and resigned.

"I didn't go all the way with her, Rose. That would be totally unfaithful. I've been lonely. Been lonely for months, even when you're with me. Lonely for companionship, even when you've been at my side. You're not mentally with me even if you're physically sitting right next to me. Isn't it obvious to you? I needed to feel like a new man again. Nothing will happen between us two . . . I mean, between me and Sarah. Nothing." He felt he lied about the last part, but wanted to spare Rose from feeling worse.

Rose's lips quivered and she began to cry. She turned away and went into the bathroom. Brandon thought she was crying because of what he did, but she was actually crying because of her evening with Stan. She *had* been totally unfaithful, and she knew she would not be able to tell Brandon anything. Not now, perhaps never. He thinks I've been faithful, she thought, and how can I live with myself? She would find a way. As a strong woman, she had always been able to face adversity and attack it and overcome it. She would need to reach down deep. Fortunately, a spell of exhaustion was cast over her. It was like a blessing from above, because she didn't want to stay awake. After a few minutes in the restroom by herself, she came out and lay in the bed without noticing Brandon and was asleep in minutes.

12

It went from bad to worse. At eight o'clock the next morning, Friday, Brandon and Rose got a call from a local hospital stating their daughter took too many pills and was in intensive care. They were going to be able to save her, but it was important they come quickly.

Brandon had just gotten out of the shower and Rose was starting to get dressed when they received this information. They were at the nearby hospital in twenty minutes. The doctor told them Brandy had called for an ambulance service either immediately before or after taking the pills so she could be rescued, and gave the phone number of where to notify her parents at the hotel.

"Unusual for this to happen in the wee hours of the morning," the emergency medical technician said. "She apparently wanted to send a message to somebody, because she definitely wanted to be rescued. It was a feigned suicide attempt. Occasionally, young people will do this. I've seen it happen before. Kids will do this to shake up their boyfriend or girlfriend who jilted them, or their best friend, or . . . their parents. She definitely wanted you to be contacted. Kids will do this to get attention from someone who normally ignores them. Usually they're very depressed. We got to her apartment in time. The front door was unlocked. She was seen on the couch with the overdose at about six-thirty this morning. We pumped her stomach. She needs to stay here awhile."

Brandon and Rose remained silent, listening intently, as they sat close to each other inside the care unit. Brandon instinctively reached over and clasped Rose's hand, doing it without really thinking, and this surprised him. She held it tightly. He felt as if the last twenty years of his life had just unrolled before his eyes and he was looking at it. The excitement of last night with both episodes of Sarah and Trevor had not even entered his mind since the phone call. Someone had just dumped a cold bucket of water over him, and he had awoken to a different life. Rose looked at him meaningfully and then gave a big sigh.

"Our beloved daughter. I can't believe it," he said.

"Hmm. I don't know what to say. She was depressed yesterday and I was concerned for her when she left me in the late afternoon. I thought she would be fine, though," Rose said forlornly.

"Is it only because of us?"

"It is partly. But it's not just us. She broke up with her boyfriend she was hoping to marry, she didn't do well in school her spring semester. . . ."

"Really?" Brandon interrupted.

"She's having trouble at work. Everything is going sour for her," Rose continued. "She did this to give us a wake-up call, and as a warning, I think."

Brandon didn't respond.

"She told me a lot of things yesterday afternoon at the beach. Things you didn't know about. The family, the one source of stability for her when everything else goes bad, she felt was crumbling, because you and I were crumbling. The family has always been a source of strength for her. With the impending divorce she would have nothing else to hold on to. It was a very dangerous thing she did, and I still can't believe she would do it, but then. . . ." Rose stopped. How could she have gone out with Stan last night after what Brandy had just relayed to her? She could no longer believe herself and what she did, so how could she question her daughter's actions? "Never mind," she said, shaking her head.

Brandon took his hand from Rose and put it over his mouth. He bowed his head, not to pray, but to contemplate deeply. Amidst his shock, he had a twinge of thankfulness the ambulance arrived on time and the doctors were able to save her. Suppose they had gone to the wrong apartment or the dosage was greater than Brandy really wanted and his daughter had left them? He wouldn't be able to conceive how he would be feeling right now. Brandon needed someone to talk this out with, and the only candidate he had was Rose.

They talked profusely over the next hour. Things they hadn't talked or reminisced about in years. Brandy's surprise birthday party when she was six, winning the spelling bee at her school when she was nine, winning the championship for her softball team with a triple at the age of eleven. These events were all impacted in both their memories. Her baptism in church when she was twelve, her first date when she was fourteen and the boy she dated, her first prom a year later. Her crushing disappointment when she broke up with her first boyfriend, her presidency of the German club, and the third-place finish at the city marathon. They brought up her excitement at becoming song leader on the cheering squad at school, and her rescuing a two-year old who was choking at a swimming pool in Yosemite. The couple felt closer to each other than at any time all week, and it was without the ocean or a sunset or some other part of nature that would always help them along so they wouldn't need to communicate. They were relating their feelings to each other about events that were meaningful to them amidst the cold, hard, colorless walls of a hospital. The couple did not feel erotic or sensuous toward each other, but shared in the mutual shock of what occurred with their own daughter and experienced a rare sense of companionship that was badly needed. Rose, during that hour, saw in Brandon a friend— and Brandon enjoyed being one, having seen in Rose a person sympathetic to the trauma he was experiencing.

They talked to Brandy later that morning. The doctor ordered some counseling, but Rose mentioned she was already seeing a therapist and would try to contact him. Brandon agreed to pay the therapist whatever it would take to help his daughter with depression. He didn't want to leave the hospital, and, along with Rose, agreed to be around for most of the remainder of the day.

They went and sat in the lounge and talked for another hour. They talked about their other three children and the many misadventures they experienced and the many more that would be coming in the future. Brandon shared a couple of family scenes of the past he recalled yesterday when at the bar. "We were a different family back then. It was just a few years ago, but seems like two lifetimes ago. What happened?"

"When things become routine, interest and excitement are lost," she said. "So sometimes change is good because it offers newness and freshness, but if things change badly, it is worse than if things had stayed routine. But, our children still love us. Shouldn't that be enough for us?"

Brandon didn't answer, and Rose didn't expect one. She thought of Sarah, whoever she was, and then of Stan. If Brandon had brought up his affair with Sarah at that time, would she be able to spill out her mess with Stan? She wanted to totally reconcile at that moment and perhaps a confession would have primed it.

Then reality sunk in, and she knew she could not tell him about the affair. Rose was not ready and she could bear the guilt.

Prior to lunch, Rose decided to go to the flower shop at the hospital and buy some flowers for Brandy. Brandon went to a payphone to call Sarah. He had promised her he would call, but had already committed himself to a very short dialogue.

"Hello Brandon, my darling, have you missed me all morning?"

Brandon felt as if he had been transported to a different life, going from a serious and relevant dialogue with Rose to hearing the erotic voice from Sarah. He could not shift gears that fast, and wasn't going to be driven off-course.

"No, I haven't," he said abruptly. "Listen, Sarah, I can't talk much to you now. I'm only calling because I said I would, and I keep my word."

"Have you been drinking? You sound awfully serious. You O.K.?"

"Yes . . . I'm . . . O.K."

"How was your business meeting this morning? Was it bad?"

"I didn't have a business meeting this morning. I'm really not here on business. I didn't tell you the truth." Brandon said this impulsively, because, at this point, he didn't care. His daughter was foremost on his mind. "I'm not really here in Hawaii on business."

"Why, you bad boy. I thought I could trust you. Hmm. What am I going to do with you?"

"Oh, I don't know," was Brandon's response. He was silent for a few seconds and he heard nothing on the other end. "Maybe you could forget me."

"Forget you! Are you kidding? Brandon, I don't like this conversation. You sound so strange . . . and serious. Last night was beautiful, it was dreamlike. Don't destroy it for me with a two minute phone call that doesn't make any sense."

"I can't really say anything more right now, Sarah. I need to go."

"But what about tonight? Can we get together tonight?"

"No we cannot. We cannot. Something bad happened this morning. And last night. . . ."

"What bad happened this morning? Tell me."

"No I can't tell you."

"Please."

"I *can't* tell you. And . . . on top of that, your brother Trevor threatened me last night after I dropped you off."

"What?"

"Yes. Yes he did. He may have been drunk, but he ran after me."

"Oh, he's as harmless as a lamb. Wouldn't hurt a flea. All bark and no bite."

"Sarah! He threatened me, do you hear?"

Sarah gave half a chuckle. "Is that what you're worried about?"

"Not just that. I've had a bad morning, and I can't talk to you about it. I can't see you tonight. And please, *please*, do not call my hotel room."

"A two-timer, huh?"

"No. It's not that." Brandon thought of telling her about Rose. "I like you, but I can't see you. Not now."

"Why did you come to Hawaii, if not for business?"

"To see Cassie. Your mother."

"Yes, I know the name of my mother."

"And you swept me off my feet. And I need to go now."

"Why, are you with someone?"

"I'm at the hospital. I can't tell you everything."

"Are you O.K.?"

"I am. I'm here to see somebody else. Can't talk about it."

"Do you still love me?" she asked in a sensuous tone.

"I can't talk anymore."

"You're supposedly leaving on the plane tomorrow. Do you still love me?"

"Sarah, please. I have to go."

"But when will I see you again? I need to see you again before you go."

"I know. And I need to go. Bye." He hung up the phone, with a struggle. Then he remembered what he was supposed to tell her. He wasn't going to see her that evening as they had planned. Did he tell her that? He couldn't remember.

He went back to the lounge and Rose had not yet returned. Perhaps she went straight from the flower shop to Brandy's bedside, Brandon thought. It would give him time to think of his options, and it certainly was much safer for him in the hospital lounge than in his hotel room. Trevor scared him, and he didn't want to be alone anywhere. After a few more minutes of reflection, including thoughts about whether he and Rose should leave tomorrow as scheduled or stay a few days longer because of Brandy, he stretched and pulled his calf muscle for the first time in three days, then got up and limped to the intensive care unit to see his daughter.

❦   ❦   ❦

"Welcome to the hospital," she said meekly, and glibly.

Brandon sighed. "Your mother and I have been under much strain today."

Brandy was silent for awhile. Then she said, "I guess it was stupid of me. I was on my last rope, and I knew you were leaving tomorrow and was worried this would be the last time I would know you as a married couple before you flew back. I was very hurt."

"We knew you felt hurt when we saw you at your apartment. It was made *very* clear. You were taking it hard. But . . . even if we were to separate, we will always . . . always still be a family."

"Don't talk of such things," Brandy said forcefully, then rolled over and turned her back to him in the bed.

Brandon walked over to the other side of the bed so he could talk into the face of his oldest daughter.

"Nothing will happen for awhile. I can promise you that. Your mother and I are going to stick it out a while longer, and . . . who knows?" He smiled calmly at her.

Brandy sighed. "I've been writing to James lately," she said, referring to her thirteen-year-old brother. "I don't know why I said that. Anyway, he loves to write, and especially to me. Why am I telling you this? I don't know."

"Does James know the troubles?"

"No. I don't think so. Lester and Jana don't either, I don't think. It would be hard for them, too."

"Yes, it would."

"Can you promise me something?" she asked, grabbing her father's hand.

This was what Brandon was afraid of. He knew it was coming and didn't surprise him.

"I don't know how good I am at keeping promises anymore, darling. I know what you want."

"Promise that you two will stay together, no matter what."

Brandon hardly heard the sentence because he knew what she would say. He closed his eyes and then bowed his head. Then he opened his eyes. "I can only promise that I will try my best." It was said with the utmost sincerity. "That's all I can tell you. You can't expect anything more from me, Brandy. I'm sure you don't want your father to live in misery. And . . . I'm sure you don't want your mother to be painfully unhappy either, do you? We will try, and I can promise you that, from both of us."

Brandy turned again, but this time lay flat on her back staring at the ceiling.

"You both don't look unhappy. When I see you both you seem fine."

"That's because when we are with you we *are* happy, because our focus is on you and not on ourselves. So . . ." Brandon stopped. He had just learned something.

"I see," she said blandly.

There was silence for a couple of minutes.

"Is there anything else I can do for you?" he asked. "Anything I can get for you?"

"I'm fine, daddy. Perhaps you can get mother."

That evening in the hotel room, Brandon couldn't sleep but noticed Rose had no problem dozing off. She had been emotionally drained, thought Brandon. Bless her. He kept tossing and turning, wondering if he would get any sleep at all. He was thinking about the other hotel they would need to move into when morning arrived, and how he would feel much safer knowing that Cassie, Sarah, and Trevor would not know where he was.

When he fell asleep, Brandon dreamed about running away from Trevor in the streets and hoping to reach his car in time to drive away. His mind was replaying the incident, hearing the screeching of brakes, and screaming. Brandon stopped running, looked back, and saw Trevor sprawled on the pavement in the middle of the intersection, his face toward the sky. A car had completely driven over him and people were coming from all directions to see the incident. Brandon walked toward the intersection, got to the front of the crowd, and noticed Trevor's bloody corpse with some broken bones, the eyes frozen open, and the mouth remaining open from his final shriek. Brandon heard murmurs from the crowd: "His chest is flat as a pancake . . . was he chasing someone? . . . Someone get his I.D. please . . . who's responsible? . . . Was it a hit-and-run?" Brandon looked at Trevor's head one last time, and then decided to get away from the crowd before anyone might apprehend him as the person Trevor was chasing. He walked to his car briskly and noticed a cold wind before reaching his car door, as if someone decided to make the outdoor temperature twenty degrees cooler by turning on a switch. He sat down in his car and was ready to turn on the ignition while closing the door, when he noticed Trevor's amputated head lying in the passenger's seat next to him, with open eyes, blinking, full of life, recognizing Brandon.

Brandon screamed, startling himself because he had never heard his voice scream in his adult life, and woke up immediately. Rose was startled, awoke, and let out a shriek herself, thinking they were being attacked by an intruder.

"Oh . . . oh . . . it's O.K. It's O.K. Rose. A nightmare," he said intensely. Rose turned on the light.

"You scared me half to death, Brandon. Honest to God!"

"I'm sorry. I'm sorry."

"I thought we were being attacked. What was the nightmare?"

"I can't tell you. I can't tell you."

He got up and walked around. Yes he couldn't tell her. But he had a sense of thankfulness that the event with Trevor was less eventful than what he had dreamed. He checked the time and it was three in the morning. At least he had gotten some sleep. Drinking a glass of wine, he eventually dozed off, but the morning alarm clock rang too quickly.

13

Saturday morning, Brandon and Rose agreed to stay in Hawaii until Tuesday or until Brandy left the hospital, whichever was later. Brandon was able to convince his wife that they should find a less expensive hotel for the remaining days as his credit line on his credit card was running thin over the last week. To leave the hotel to a place more clandestine where his college sweetheart Cassie and her voluptuous daughter and maniacal son could not contact him would not be too soon for Brandon.

It was eight-thirty that morning when the phone rang while Brandon was drinking his coffee out in the balcony and Rose was in the shower. Brandon answered the phone, and it was Cassie.

"I'll need to talk to you later," Brandon said nervously. "I'll call you."

"No. You're going to talk to me, *now*."

"No I'm not. Cassie, I can't talk to you now. I'll call you. I promise."

"I just need to ask you one question. Is it true. . . ?

Brandon hung up the phone. He went back out to the balcony and finished his coffee.

Rose came out of the shower five minutes later.

"Who was that?" Rose asked as she dried herself with a towel.

"It was the front desk reminding us we had until twelve o'clock to check out."

"But . . . they've never done that before."

"What do you mean? We've never been at this hotel before in Hawaii."

"I mean, I haven't heard a hotel calling like that on the last day."

"Well, it's bad public relations to the customers if they have to charge them for an extra day if they don't check out in time."

Rose went back into the bathroom and dried her hair with a blow-dryer.

Brandon began thinking about his children, and suddenly realized he was truly missing them. He did not feel this way two days ago.

His immediate family was truly in the forefront of his thoughts now.

After conferring with Rose, they called home and told the children they would not be coming back home that evening, but they would need to wait for them to come home next week, Tuesday at the earliest. They talked to each of the three, the youngest of the three the most disappointed. Brandon didn't mention about Brandy's hospitalization, and fortunately they didn't ask about her.

After contacting his work about "unforeseen problems" and Brandy's hospitalization, he got permission to stay an extra week away from his job. He and Rose then checked out of the hotel and went to the hospital to see Brandy.

They checked in to a new place that afternoon and then laid out on the beach at Waikiki. Both were not passionate, but felt companionship amidst new topics of conversation. They each did not want to be alone because of the shock created by Brandy's ordeal. Brandon and Rose continued to need each other during this time. And when sunset was approaching, they tried to guess the number of minutes it would be before the sun went below the horizon. It helped to pass the time of day, and passing the time of day was important because each felt stronger the longer time progressed from the previous day's news about their daughter. Brandon and Rose, normally so independent of the other, were giving each other emotional strength and showed how weak and vulnerable during a time of trauma each of them were without the other.

The vacation, which was to be seven days, was supposed to be over. The couple recalled how they were feeling on the airplane last Saturday. Now they were starting the epilogue. Or was this past week's journey a prelude to a longer, bigger, and better journey?

It wasn't until Monday morning when the hospital called and said Brandy would be released from her stay at three in the afternoon. Brandon scheduled a flight to Los Angeles for the following morning. He and Rose had been in and out of the hospital over the weekend a number of times to check up on their daughter.

Early that afternoon, Brandon went out for a walk from his new hotel and went into the flower shop to see Sarah. It was only about a fifteen minute walk. He had already played out in his mind the dialogue he intended to have with her, as well as the fortitude to keep his sexual emotions in check. He *needed* to see her.

He saw her walk in to the shop as he was approaching from the other side of the street. She was just getting back from lunch, he thought. He went inside and she saw him immediately. Sarah gasped, and put her hands over her mouth. After a few seconds, she walked up to him while he was standing still only a few feet in front of the entrance.

"Brandon. Brandon, my sweet. Why are you still here? I thought I had lost you forever. Weren't you to leave on Saturday?"

"We decided to stay until Tuesday."

"Who's we?"

Brandon hesitated. Then said, "My business partner."

"I thought you told me Friday on the phone from the hospital you weren't here on business."

Brandon took a deep breath. "That's right. I did say that, didn't I?" He sighed as she looked glaringly at him. "I was staying with a fellow from my company's Honolulu office. I was visiting the Honolulu office to see how they were doing with their computerized accounting procedures. But it was on my vacation time."

"But why would a fellow from the Honolulu office be staying with you at the hotel? If he works at that office he must live in the vicinity, right?"

"Yes . . . well . . . we had to work together after his office hours."

"Work or play?"

"Sarah . . . enough!" This was not the dialogue Brandon had even come close to planning. He composed himself. "Listen, Sarah, I . . . am very fond of you. I'm sure you know that. I'm leaving tomorrow morning by plane and I want to thank you for the great times we had together, even though there were some embarrassing moments. Such as when your mother walked in on us."

Sarah didn't smile or frown. Brandon waited for her to say something, but she didn't.

"I don't want you to call me when I get back into the L.A. area. Please don't call. Don't try to find my phone number. I won't respond."

"Work or play? I still haven't gotten an answer. That man you claimed you were with." She was teasing him, and being serious with him. Her face depicted both.

"Honestly, Sarah. If you really think I'm bisexual, you wouldn't want to be involved with me anyway. So don't contact me. Wait for me to contact you, if ever."

"Oh, I don't think there was ever a man with you," Sarah said, rather amused. "I know it's a woman. A woman always knows when there's another woman. *Eventually* she does."

"Then if you think that, you wouldn't want to be involved with my life when there's another woman, right? If that's what you think. And if you think I'm a liar . . . well, you shouldn't want to be a part of me."

"I do think you are having an affair, and you are a perpetual romantic. It would be best for you if you would just settle down. You know how much I adore you. I know I'm the perfect one for you to settle down with. I think you love me, and I think you know it too . . . but, on the other hand, I wish you would learn to just tell me the truth about things. That *is* a problem." She appeared relaxed, but Brandon saw that inside of her she was very intense. Sarah was able to look at Brandon with the same fondness he saw when she looked at him on the sands of the beach just a few nights before.

"Sarah, you have a customer," said a voice from behind the cash register that obviously belonged to a supervisor.

Sarah turned around and immediately walked to the customer who was looking at some orchids.

While she was conversing with the person, Brandon realized this would be the best time for his getaway. But he didn't want to leave. Then he thought again. What else was there to tell her? He told her he was very fond of her, thanked her for the good times, and told her not to contact him. There was nothing more. He made a quick u-turn out the door, and then forced himself to keep walking toward his hotel. The longer he walked the harder it was for him, but the stronger his will became.

It wasn't until he reached his room and sat down with a beer that he regretted the last words he might ever hear from the sweet mouth of Sarah: "that *is* a problem." And he didn't kiss her goodbye, or give her a hug. His time with her was only a couple of minutes, not ten. He decided to look at it rationally, not emotionally, and realized it was for the best.

Rose was with Stan at about the same time of the afternoon. The bar where they met was also within walking distance of the hotel.

Rose, in a similar fashion as her husband, also wanted the meeting to be short. She was not as successful.

Rose told him she couldn't see him anymore.

"You've said that before," Stan said loudly, too loud for the intimate atmosphere of the bar.

"Sh. Please, Stan. Listen to me. I have guilt to deal with."

"No you don't."

"Are you telling me what I feel and what I don't feel?"

"Divorce him. You know it won't work."

"Do you care about our oldest daughter? No you don't."

"Look. You two have gotten along well over the weekend because you have a mutual bond with your daughter and what she tried to do to herself. Or, rather, what she tried to get you to think she was going to do to herself. But it won't last. You can't have your kids trying suicide every week of the year in order to keep you two together."

"You don't care at all about her, or the children, do you?" Rose said rather angrily. "If I were to have a permanent relationship with a man, that man would need to learn to like and respect my kids."

Stan was silent.

"Brandon doesn't know anything about this," continued Rose. "I may tell him soon. I feel bad that he doesn't, because he thinks I've been faithful to him. . . all of these years. And I have been faithful . . . most of the time."

Stan grabbed her hands in his.

"I know you've gone through a lot, Rose. I'm sorry for not being compassionate toward your children at this very moment. Right now, I want *you*. The relationship I intend to have with your children will work itself out later on. I know it will."

"But they love their father."

Stan started to speak and then stopped. Rose took her hands away from Stan's.

"I'm so captivated by you I don't care about anyone or anything else," Stan said in an intense whisper.

"Then you will need to start," she whispered back. "Brandon and I need to think of the kids. We need to wait until after our children have left the house before we do anything drastic."

"When will that be?"

"Our youngest is thirteen."

Stan shrugged, and rolled his eyes.

"This is very hard for me, don't you understand?" Rose continued. "I'm very fond of you. I need more time, a lot more time. Give me that freedom. Time heals."

"Time heals love? What is love to you, a disease?" Stan said, raising his voice.

"Dishonest love. Love that shouldn't be there."

"You know that Brandon hasn't been faithful either," Stan said with his eyebrows raised. "What was her name? The one he was rolling around in the hay with? Sarah?"

"Yes, Sarah. And based on the sound of her voice on the telephone, she's probably twenty years younger."

"Hmm. A bad situation."

"Got to go, Stan."

"Wasn't our sex wonderful last Thursday night?"

"Yes. Wonderful. Will never forget it. And I got to go." Rose stood up and began exiting. He followed her before she reached the door, turned her around, and then kissed her passionately on the lips. Rose complied. Then she looked into his eyes intently.

"Goodbye, Stan." She was out the door.

❦   ❦   ❦

Brandon and Rose met Brandy at the hospital that afternoon at three, and took her back to her apartment. Brandon made arrangements with her therapist she had been seeing, telling his daughter he would take care of the payments from now until she felt comfortable without a therapist.

The couple spent the early evening laying out on the beach and watching another sunset. They didn't talk much, but enjoyed the setting that had been made-to-order for them. Emotionally exhausted, they went to bed early.

After a good visit with Brandy at her apartment the following morning, Brandon and Rose were on a jet airliner for Los Angeles. Both had so much to think about when they flew home, and remained relatively quiet. Each spent time thinking what the other was thinking. Both were unsure of the future, and would face the prospects in a low-key manner as to what each new day would bring. Brandon felt he was starting a new chapter in life, while Rose felt she was finishing one.

14

It was twenty-five years later and Brandon was lying in his hammock with some cool wind blowing in his face. He and Rose were up at their Big Bear Lake cabin for a week's get away from their busier life in Upland. She was getting groceries and Brandon had a lazy mood because of the lazy atmosphere. He swayed the hammock back-and-forth a little and used his memory of important events in his life to entertain himself. Having already retired from the advertising agency, he was not burdened with work but lived off of his retirement and was spending more time with his children and grandchildren. This particular time up in the mountains, however, was meant for the couple to be spent on each other.

He remembered when he first met Rose forty-six years ago in a judicial office. It had been the most unusual way to meet, but he was never accustomed to the routine anyway. He and Rose were appealing their parking tickets, received from a different police officer but for the same reason: parking in a no-parking zone on a Monday morning because of street cleaning. They each received their tickets for the same city block in Los Angeles, even though the tickets were two weeks apart. Both claimed they couldn't see the no-parking sign because it was covered by the foliage and branches of a tree. Each took pictures of the tree for their proof. A parking administrator who answered appeals decided to bring them both into his office and handle the claims at the same time. He reluctantly reversed both tickets, and after leaving his office the couple found a liking to each other. They talked incessantly afterward, and Brandon asked her to lunch for the following day and the relationship had a crescendo up to the wedding the next year. Brandon would joke with his four children telling them they owed their existence to the foliage of the tree on that particular city block.

After departing from Hawaii twenty-five years ago, Brandon always had second thoughts about remaining with Rose. Rose was extremely quiet toward Brandon during those first months after that critical seven-day vacation that turned into ten. Brandon didn't see a way to continue the marriage but couldn't see a way out, and used his children as an excuse to stay in it.

He liked the idea of playing-the-field with women if he was single again. His short time with Sarah was still in his thoughts, as well as other possible rendezvous he could have. But that lifestyle had its liabilities. And as a married man, that lifestyle was not only immoral to him—he had always thought that—but it could create far more problems than joys. His marriage had been only lukewarm-happy, and the temptation to jump the fence would come and go. Rose, he thought, had always been faithful and never cheated on him, and she deserved a husband who kept his behavior in check. Staying with Rose was only a consistent "C+" experience, but he opted to stay with her, and maybe it was because of the stability he wanted in his life. His marriage would always be there for him.

Brandon's ability to stay away from extra-marital affairs over these years was two-pronged. Either he was able to stop the affair from starting in its tracks, or else outside events beyond his control prevented an affair from developing. An example of the first case occurred several months after the couple came home from that vacation week in Hawaii. Their marriage counselor encouraged the couple to get together with other couples who were friends with them, and go to places together. They selected Gary and Margaret, whom they had met at a luau during that vacation week. Margaret invited them to come up to see their mountain home in Lake Tahoe whenever they were in the vicinity. After some skiing in the Mammoth area, Brandon and Rose dropped by to see their home, then the four went to dinner at a restaurant. They had interesting conversation during dinner as each couple had four children, and Brandon was in the same line of work as Gary. But Brandon noticed Margaret intensely looking at him every ten seconds and made him shift in his seat often, giving him the look of being restless. After the steak dinner and dessert Brandon got up to go to the restroom, and when he came out, Margaret was there to greet him.

"When are you skiing again at Mammoth?" she asked.

"Oh, I don't really know. Maybe next spring."

"My husband doesn't like to ski." Brandon could smell the champagne on her breath. He also had had two glasses himself. "Actually, you could come up here to Tahoe and ski," she continued and put her right hand in his hip pocket, "but it would be in the watchful eye of my husband. We wouldn't want that, would we?"

"I plan to be up in Mammoth next . . . look, no thanks. Please."

"You know you want it."

Brandon noticed they were all alone in the hallway. "Wanting it doesn't mean it's the right thing."

"You know you want it. Gary will be away on a business trip in three weekends from now. He's going to St. Louis, and how about that?"

"You should go with him."

"I noticed that Rose is very cold to you. Not exciting. Is she as dull at home as in a restaurant?"

"Rose and I have been through a lot and we're working on our relationship and trying to restore. . . ." He stopped, and worried that Rose might need to use the restroom also.

"You're working? At your relationship? Love is work?"

"Please, Margaret. Not now."

"Then when?" She took her hand out of his pocket, and briefly caressed his crotch before he backed away.

"We've had too much champagne," he said.

"Here is my business card," Margaret said, putting the card in his shirt pocket. "Don't let it fall out. Why then, Rose might see it and only be about ten percent as jealous as a wife would normally be." She stroked his cheek and then gave him a quick kiss on the lips. "Remember, three weeks. I'll wait for your call."

"Don't do this, you attractive. . . ."

"Don't act like a wounded puppy when what you really are is a dog on the prowl. Ruff, ruff!"

"Sh!" he cautioned her, but smiled. "Quiet."

"No one will hear us. And why are you looking out at the table? Your wife is out on the patio. She can't see us."

"And your husband?"

"He's out on the patio with her, I think." She laughed.

"This has gone long enough."

"I think you get my drift. I'm extremely attracted to you, and I know you're playing hard to get, which makes me want to prance all over you, and I'm sure you're just wonderful in bed, and I'm just going to have to wait for you when you're sober I guess. . . ."

She hugged him, and then he left her to go find Rose. He found her alone smoking a cigarette out on the patio. The foursome eventually worked their way back to the table again. Brandon felt terribly excited and wished to be single again. Margaret kept glancing over at him, smiling, and Brandon returned the glances with a straight face. He then thought of Brandy out of the clear thin air, and remembered the facial expression she had in the hospital as he spoke to her. Brandon remembered that restaurant scene vividly, including the dialogue with Margaret word for word. He never called her, and destroyed the business card. She left a message on his office phone two weeks later hoping she could convince him to come north, but he didn't respond. He never heard from her again. In looking back, Brandon was proud of the way he took care of himself that evening.

A year and a few months after this incident, there was an example of how a peripheral event beyond his control prevented him from renewing an affair. It was Brandy's graduation from the University of Hawaii. The time was early June. Two weeks prior to the graduation, he was skiing in Mammoth, the spring snow still full and able to accommodate the skiers. He broke his leg in two places when he tried the expert run after already being tired with five hours of skiing. He was going too fast, lost traction on some ice, and landed badly. It was the first and only time he ever broke a bone. He had to miss the graduation in Hawaii, as it would only be troublesome for him to get around. Rose took the camcorder, and he was able to see the motion picture of the event when she returned home.

He noticed in the graduation program that his daughter received the same degree with the same major, journalism, as Sarah Logan. It caught him by surprise, although it shouldn't have because he should have remembered. When he visited Hawaii two years previous, Sarah was about the same age as Brandy and also had the same major going to the same school. He noticed from the program roster that only seven graduated majoring in journalism. Did Sarah know Brandy as his daughter? Damn. He told her the name of his eldest during the lunch hour at her house, but would she have remembered it? Sarah knew his last name was Peeters, but he never told her that Brandy was majoring in journalism or where she went to school. Did she blab to Brandy about the affair? He would never be able to get himself to ask his daughter if she knew Sarah personally. It would only get her to be inquisitive and then she would ask Sarah how she knew her dad. He would always wonder if Brandy knew of the affair, and it was another punishment he would endure for his misdeed. Did Sarah relay the affair to Brandy and cause the suicide attempt? Brandon turned in his hammock and thought to himself a definite "no." Brandy was not in school that summer and there was no reason for Sarah, at least as far as that week was concerned, to have communicated anything to his daughter. Whether she relayed information to his daughter after that time was something he would never know.

Brandon *did* know for sure that had he gone to the graduation he would have definitely found a way to talk to Sarah at that time, whether it be in private or public. And with his emotions running high, his mind sporadically thinking about this beautiful nymph over those two previous years, Brandon would have been unrestrained as to how far he would have gone with her. But because of a freak accident on a ski slope and circumstances beyond his control, this meeting was detoured. It was better not to see his daughter graduate, than to have seen her and perhaps wreck the marriage because of her schoolmate.

Brandon stretched on the hammock, having finally learned how not to pull his calf muscle, and his thoughts turned to Cassie. The last he heard of her was a telephone call to his office at work a week after he left Hawaii. It was basically a monologue, with Cassie unconcerned about any response from Brandon.

She spoke calmly but very straightforward. "Sarah has not told me all the details about you two, but I got a good idea with what I saw in my living room when I unexpectedly came home during lunch. Because she's twenty, I can't legally stop anything you do. Trevor found you two together near Sarah's car in Honolulu when I sent him to the drug store to find out why Sarah was so long in getting the prescriptions. I have Trevor under control, don't worry about him. If he harms or threatens you in *any* way, contact me and I'm throwing him out of the house. That would be disastrous for him because he hasn't been able to hold a job for more than a month. He's lucky to get through his one class a semester without being thrown out of the class by the teacher for disturbing the students. Now, Brandon, regarding you—please, please stay away from my daughter. She doesn't know what she gets herself into half the time. An extremely intelligent girl, but naive. She fell. She fell for you. I'm fond of you—always will be—and you're a perpetual romantic at heart. I found out that you are *still* married and I told Sarah this." Brandon grunted. Sarah must be really hurt. "You lied to me. We're at different places in our lives. You're married, and I'm here in Hawaii and don't wish to leave. Plus your seducement of my daughter kind of put a major dent in any future affair or relationship between us, don't you agree? I'm aware she looks like I did when I was her age, but that is beside the point. Kindly, stay away from her. I wish you happiness and success, Brandon."

"Let me just say . . ." he started, but then she hung up.

He had no idea to this day what happened with her or Sarah. A quarter of a century has passed and how time has flown, and flown much too quickly. Still living? Married? Happy or sad? He knew nothing, and he had already decided years ago that Hawaii was off-limits. Brandon knew about his passions well, and would look up Sarah in no time if she were in a few miles radius of him. He had learned that if he stretched his passions too far, he and others would get hurt, much like the stretching of his calf muscle.

Brandon turned on his side and thought he might get in a nap. He pondered about his kids and grandchildren, the fruits and rewards of a marriage. Brandy is now forty-four, happily married with three children. She works as a journalist for a magazine in New York City. Jana, two years younger, was in her second marriage after an early marriage ended in a quick divorce. She has a seven-year-old that is in a Montessori school. Her job is in cosmetics, and lives near Fresno. Lester just turned forty, amazing, and is also in his second marriage after his first wife died of a brain tumor. No kids, and works for the Whittier Police Department. Then there is wonderful James, the youngest. He has never married, and is the most financially successful of all. Airline pilot, and has done well with the stock market. Money just piles up. He keeps in touch with his mom and dad more than the other three put together. The last time the entire family was together occurred two Christmases ago, and Brandon wished it could happen more often.

Rose drove back with the groceries preventing him from dozing off. He got out of his comfort place on the hammock and helped her bring the groceries into the cabin. Then he got back on the hammock again, and knew Rose would soon be near him sitting on her rocking chair.

15

❀

Rose moved her rocking chair forward and back. She smiled and relaxed.

"Did you doze off?" she asked.

"No. I was too engrossed in thinking about us," Brandon responded.

"Us?"

"When we first met."

"You mean, in the judicial office?"

"Yes."

"Goodness, Brandon, that was three lifetimes ago."

"I know. It was the extra foliage on the tree that did it."

"Brandon, you know as well as I do that we would have met some other way if not *that* way."

"Maybe. Maybe not. Our trips to Hawaii, the kids growing up. Brandy's graduation that I missed. The grandchildren."

"It's been a long, long road," she said.

Yes it had, thought Brandon. Sometimes bumpy, sometimes smooth. He had to be satisfied with that.

Rose had never confessed to Brandon her affair with Stan, and it had caused her much guilt. She knew Brandon did not have a problem with guilt because he confessed to his wayward plight, and seen by Rose exactly for what he was. They both miscued on that vacation week but she could not get herself to tell Brandon what happened, and because he always looked at her as the totally faithful wife of forty-five years, Rose bore the guilt she would always carry.

She analyzed further that it made Brandon happy he had married a totally faithful wife for that long a period. Why break his happiness? Was her wish for his happiness greater than the release of her guilt? Men had such egos, and for a man to know he had been cheated on made him feel half-emasculated because his lover found someone better. At this stage, why bother telling him?

Or was it for selfish reasons? Perhaps she didn't tell him because she felt good with him thinking he had the perfect faithful wife. She didn't want to give that up, even if giving that up meant releasing her guilt by telling him the truth. Either way, she could look back at all the years and realize she had done all right the majority of the time. She last miscued when she got together with Stan a couple of days after Brandy's graduation in Hawaii when Brandon was at home with his broken leg. That was twenty-three years ago. She remembered the scene vividly.

Stan said the same trite and unchangeable overtures to her. "Please stay. I love you and how you feel, your warmth, your movements, everything about you." He said these same words like a robot when he was inside her at the motel. She had consented. And she did feel that he loved her, but didn't love the way Brandon did. Rose had the sexual passionate love for Stan but not the companionship love as she did for her husband.

"What am I going to do?" she asked when their love play was over.

"Do you love me?"

"Yes."

"Just enjoy, don't analyze. You always *analyze*."

"I can't help it."

"Yes you can help it," Stan said annoyingly. "When you analyze, it cheapens what we did."

"You aren't married. I still have my children to think about. You have no baggage with you when we go to bed together."

"Leave your baggage outside," he said irritatingly.

Rose sat up in bed as Stan got up from her. She began to get dressed, and they didn't speak for a minute. Rose was deep in thought. Stan was so shallow. He only talks about me and about nothing else, like a trained parrot. At least Brandon was multi-faceted and would talk to her on a range of issues: traveling, baseball, different kinds of coffee, magazines, skiing, remodeling the house, advertising, nature, gardening, to name a few. He was far more interesting than this predictable, boring specimen of a man that could only talk about her and how "captivating" she was. It is not good for a man to be controlled by another like that. She liked an independent man, and her appreciation for Brandon swept into her like a flood.

"O.K., I will leave my baggage outside," she said, as she finished getting dressed. "And I am going to go outside with it. For good." She had made up her mind. It was all over. She couldn't continue with a husband and children in the background. Rose left the room and never saw him again.

"The wind feels so good," Brandon said, interrupting her thoughts. "It is blowing just right. It moves the hammock a little."

"What else were you thinking about, my love?" asked Rose.

"Oh . . . so many things. Our trips to Hawaii. The time that I had a little miscue. You remember?"

"A what? Miscue? Oh, you mean that. What was her name? Sarah?"

"Yes, Sarah. I was such a fool. You still half-forgive me, right?"

"Half-forgiveness is not really forgiveness. I forgive you, and don't worry about it."

"And then Brandy that same week did something not so smart either."

"Yes. That was a low point."

"I don't know why I am bringing these things up. We're happy now."

"Yes, we're happy now," she said, and watched him look at her, the perfect faithful wife. She was ready to say it. Rose stopped rocking. She was going to tell him. Now. Yes, now. It was on the tip of her tongue. She could feel her heart beat faster. He wasn't going to say anything more, and she was going to say something next. She would just say, "I cheated on you also that week, with Stan. Remember your buddy, the one who used to work for your outfit? The guy we went on a helicopter ride with in Hawaii with his wife ten years before? I did . . . I had sex with him. I shouldn't have done that." And then all her guilt would be gone and she would feel ten pounds lighter on each shoulder. Or *would* it all be gone? Rose stopped herself. She couldn't get herself to say it. And if she told him, he may think she had cheated with other men as well, and how would she be able to disprove it to him? Rose began rocking again.

Brandon looked at her and felt truly happy that he was married to her. He could not remember a time when he had loved her more than he did at that moment.

"You want to go roller skating?" Brandon asked.

"Why, you bring up the most unusual things all of a sudden. Is there a rink around here?"

"I know there is at Blue Jay for ice skating in the winter. There must be a rink for roller skating in the summer. Either ice skating or roller skating will be fine with me."

"I'll need to give that some thought."

"Don't you want to see me fall on my can, and have everyone around me laugh at a sixty-seven year-old man?"

"I think you want to see *me* fall."

"Well maybe we could fall together," he said rather excitedly. "You know. We'll be skating, holding hands, balancing pretty well, and then I'll say one-two-three fall, and we purposefully fall down together, and then everyone will see us and either laugh or go out to help us, or maybe even call for an ambulance. We'll be the center of attention. Would you like that?"

"Sounds like a plan," Rose said, rather excitedly. "But, we'll *need* to fall together. If one of us falls before the other one does, it will wreck it. We would have to do it together."

"Great. I'll check a newspaper pretty soon and find a rink."

Brandon stretched cautiously without pulling his calf, and changed his position in the hammock. Rose continued rocking, looking at Brandon with a lukewarm smile.

SHORT STORIES

ESCAPADES

"Hello, Calvin," answered Sylvia to her husband who called on the phone. It was ten-thirty at night. "Caught up in another party?"

"No, I'm not going to a party. The director needs to get together with me right now for about half an hour. We're going to a cafe to have coffee. You wanted me to call you at this time whenever I'm going to be late coming home after the show. Remember?"

Calvin was an expert makeup artist during the 1950's at the downtown playhouse, in an Alabama city of about eight thousand.

"Yes, I remember," said Sylvia. "Where are you calling from?"

"A pay phone," answered Calvin. "The play went real well tonight. There was a good audience. More sophisticated."

"Good." Sylvia was quiet for a few seconds. "So, when will you be home?"

"When the director gets through with me. I don't know when that will be. Perhaps around eleven-thirty at the latest."

A discouraged sigh came from Sylvia that Calvin could hear on the phone.

"It's part of the job, Sylvia. When we moved here we agreed that this job would help supplement my other income. There's no other way. And I enjoy doing this kind of work. Now . . . " A gunshot stopped Calvin from speaking.

Sylvia heard the gunshot over the phone and heard the receiver drop as well.

"Calvin," said Sylvia nervously. She waited for Calvin to reply. "Calvin." She heard a clump on the phone as if a body had fallen. "Calvin!" she screamed. Another gunshot was heard.

"My dear, what's wrong?" shouted Thelma, who was sitting at the table in Sylvia's home. They had been playing cards.

"No. Oh, no, I don't believe it." Sylvia hung up the phone. "Someone has shot Calvin!"

Thelma gasped.

"Thelma, call the police quick!" Sylvia shrieked. "I'm driving down to the playhouse. Tell them my husband has been shot from a local pay phone." She flew out the door.

Calvin and Sylvia Potter had arrived in their new home town four weeks prior to the fatal shooting. They had been married five years, and it was the second marriage for both. Calvin worked nightly at the playhouse. Being one of the few playhouses in the county, people would come for miles around to see the plays. It was the one thing the city took great pride in.

Calvin was in his mid-fifties and was almost entirely bald. But he applied for the job with a nice dark toupee and looked fifteen years younger and very attractive. He showed up at the rehearsals and performances with his toupee and no one working for the theatre company knew about his bald head. Sylvia never saw him with his toupee because he was always backstage if she was in the audience.

It didn't take Calvin very long to get attracted to another lady after he got his new theatre job. He started seeing Lucy Downs, who was a costume designer for the playhouse. Calvin told Lucy he wasn't married. He would come over to her house after the play the evenings that her husband, Sam, a mechanic who worked at the auto shop in town, was out at the billiard parlor. The parlor was open until midnight and was the only place in town besides the playhouse and cafe that would be open late. Sam would usually shoot billiards three times a week and would never be home before midnight so those nights gave Calvin some time to be with Lucy. Calvin would not dare to be seen with Lucy in public for fear of being apprehended by his wife, his wife's friends, Sam, or gossipers. Her home, which was only two blocks from the theatre, was the only place to see her.

The night Calvin was murdered he was not in a phone booth but at Lucy's home calling from her bedroom phone. She was lying on the bed, fully clothed, while Calvin sat on the bed with the phone talking to his wife.

Lucy had insisted to Sam that he go to the billiard parlor more often and stay as long as he liked in order to release his nervous energy from his day's work at the shop. Because of Lucy's urging to stay late, Sam left the billiard parlor early that evening, convinced she might be with someone. When he walked in at ten-thirty, he heard Calvin's lies on the phone, then in a fit of rage grabbed his rifle from the cupboard and shot him in the head. Lucy didn't scream, but put her hands to her face. Calvin fell on the ground. Another shot followed.

"You should have known I might do something like this, you cheat!" screamed Sam to Lucy. He put a hand to his heart as if he was about to have a cardiac arrest, then sat down and began to feel calmer. Sam then went through a discourse about the vices of adultery and infidelity as if their bedroom had turned into a church while forgetting his act of murder.

"You'll get life in jail for this," sobbed Lucy.

"Not if nobody knows about it," said Sam, standing up. "You won't tell anybody will you? You make a peep and I'll come back after you and do the same thing to you, do you hear? I don't love you anymore. You don't mean a thing to me. Now clean up the blood off the floor while I drag this guy into the trunk of my car."

Lucy remained motionless. He put a towel around Calvin's head and dragged him out of the room and outside. She eventually cleaned up the mess. He put Calvin's body in the trunk of his car.

He came back in the house. "Is anybody expecting him home tonight?"

Lucy hesitated. "No. He lives alone. He isn't married."

"That's good. I'm spending one more night here. Then I'm leaving you. I'll pack tomorrow and be out of your sight by tomorrow evening. The body will be safe in the trunk. Tomorrow night I'll bury him somewhere. And you keep your mouth shut." He used his index finger to emphasize every word to her.

"Yes sir," she said to her husband.

"This bed in here is mine," he said sternly. "You sleep out here on the couch." He then went to bed feeling everything was safe.

When the police received the phone call from Thelma, they immediately found Sylvia near the playhouse walking around looking for pay phones. The police searched all of the pay phone booths in the city and found nothing.

The next morning, Sylvia showed herself to be somewhat hysterical in front of the police when they questioned about her husband. They tried to calm her but it was impossible. In the early afternoon she looked inside the phone booths of the city, hoping to find any evidence of the shooting, such as blood stains. The police calmly told her to expect the worst. Two gunshots would easily kill her husband if he was hit where a gunman would usually aim. But she told the police she had not given up hope and thought he could still be alive. She reminded them that he wore a dark toupee when he was working at the theatre company. The theatrical company was shocked about the shooting and had to hire someone from another county to sub for that evening's performance.

The police asked Sylvia if he had any new enemies in town since his arrival, and whether he got along with the people he worked with. She said she didn't know. Any extra-marital affairs? She said she didn't know that either.

It was now eight o'clock in the evening, one night after the fatal shooting. It was dark. Sam Downs was riding in his car with Sylvia. Calvin was in the trunk, no less dead than the previous evening. They were driving out of the town to a motel in the country about fifty miles away. While Lucy was out of the house that afternoon, Sam packed everything he needed to escape with Sylvia, who also was able to pack everything in the late afternoon.

"Soon we'll be married," said Sam excitedly.

After Sam's divorce proceedings with Lucy were completed, he wanted to marry Sylvia as soon as possible, preferably in Las Vegas.

"Yes, at last," said Sylvia. "Well, I've never been in the theatre but I've had to do more acting these last twenty-four hours than I've had to do in my whole life."

"Did you say you had a witness to the phone call?"

"Yes. I made sure Thelma was there so she could call the police and witness how upset I was over my husband's shooting. Then today I acted hysterical in front of the police and they saw me check all the phone booths so they knew how agitated I was. They'll never suspect me. I even told them that I still had hope my husband was still alive."

"That's smart," said Sam. "Well that's the whole reason why we had to wait a day before escaping."

"Well, you were the mastermind. You set up just about everything," said Sylvia.

"I almost didn't make it to my house at ten-thirty last night. I got in just in time. And Calvin called right on time like you said he probably would."

"I would have prolonged the conversation on the phone until I heard the gunshot. When I heard it go off I acted crazy but deep inside I thought to myself, 'now I'm free'."

Calvin had always promised Sylvia he would call at ten-thirty if he was going to be late getting home. As long as Sam told Lucy he was going to stay until twelve at the parlor, Sylvia knew that Calvin would try to spend as much time as he could with Lucy, undoubtedly at her home where he would be undetected.

"Everything worked out so beautifully." Sylvia said smiling. "I'm going to miss the parlor where we first met."

"Yes, I know," said Sam. "It was pure luck. You only came into the parlor because you were lonely, with Calvin always being at the playhouse every night. He never knew about it."

"I have no sympathy for him at all. I know he's been messing around with other women for the last two years."

"I know how you feel. I knew Lucy was doing something, but had no evidence until you told me. It's amazing that you two met up."

Sylvia and Lucy were friends in high school, and met again years later at the downtown beauty salon three weeks ago. They started talking, and Lucy mentioned she was seeing a makeup artist at the playhouse. At first, Sylvia didn't believe it was Calvin because Lucy said he had dark hair, but then remembered about the toupee. When Lucy mentioned about the mannerisms he had, then Sylvia knew it was her husband.

"I never let her know that he was my husband," Sylvia told Sam. "I told you of course before that she thinks he's unmarried. When I found out he was unfaithful, I thought to myself that I don't deserve this, and of course you came along."

Sam put his arm around her.

"Well hopefully it will be smooth sailing from here on in, babe," said Sam.

"Is Lucy sworn to secrecy regarding this murder? I mean, I'm not worried about myself, I'm getting away scot-free. But what about you?"

"Don't worry about me," said Sam. "I told Lucy if she blabs anything, she's going to get the same thing from me. She knows I don't love her. But . . . I wouldn't kill her, even though she thinks I would. She has too many friends in town. People would get suspicious of me. But with Calvin, he's relatively new in town. And although he's known at the playhouse, we've done it is so good that as long as Lucy doesn't blab, we're clear. I don't believe anyone at the playhouse knew that Calvin was involved with the costume designer. I think he wanted to keep it a secret."

"Yes, you're right. Word can get around fast." Sylvia was quiet for a few seconds, and then said, "I love you, Sam. I can't wait to get to the motel." They were now very close to each other in the car. "We're going to throw Calvin in that small lake you mentioned before we spend the night, aren't we?"

"I don't know. It's not late enough. We'll be at the motel within an hour. It's called Murphy's motel. After we get moved in, let's play around first, and then dump Calvin. I want to make sure it's very late before we get rid of him. I want to make sure we can't be apprehended."

"Did you say the lake is only about a half mile behind the motel?" asked Sylvia.

"About. Don't worry. The motel is on the main road but way out in the boondocks, and we may be the only ones lodging there. Next to the motel is a dirt road that leads to a coffee plantation. The road ends, but beyond that, behind a hill, there's a small hidden lake."

They arrived at Murphy's motel at nine. Sam paid for a room in cash. Sylvia had convinced him she would register the room under a fictitious name, as they didn't want anyone to know where they were or anything about their elopement. She was also trying to convince him to dump Calvin immediately after they moved in, instead of his idea of sneaking out in the wee hours of the morning to do it. Sylvia said she wanted to get it over with.

After moving in their luggage, Sam insisted on having a bite to eat at the cafe, which was part of the hotel. Sylvia relented, but seemed nervous.

"I'm starved," said Sam. "I need to eat now. Don't worry, don't worry. Everything's going to work out fine. Look, no one knows us out here, O.K.? I know you want to dispose of Calvin quickly, but it will only take us about ten minutes, altogether. I've checked out the place. There's a short pier that can take us out into the middle of the water. The pier was used for fishing at one time, but nobody fishes there anymore. Nobody knows about the place. He'll never be found if no one ever suspects that he's there. Relax."

The waiter at the cafe was also the hotel reception clerk. As Sam and Sylvia were also to learn during the meal, he was also the owner of the hotel, Charles Murphy. The chef was also the custodian. Sam and Sylvia did not see any other workers. It was a one-story four room motel with the cafe.

After the meal, they went back to their room, then out to the car. They drove on a dirt road to the end, and then continued driving on grass until they reached the small lake. After making sure they were alone, they opened the trunk. Sylvia saw Calvin in his toupee and laughed nervously.

"I always wanted to know what he looked like with that on. He looks a lot younger. More attractive," she said.

"You didn't see him at the playhouse?" asked Sam.

"No. He was always backstage," said Sylvia.

"That's right. Well, shall we throw him in with the toupee on or off?"

"Leave it on. We don't want a trace of him."

They wrapped Calvin in a sheet as a precaution against leaving blood stains somewhere, and carried him out to the end of the pier. Sylvia and Sam each had one end of Calvin. "One, two, three!!" they counted, and then launched Calvin into the cool water.

They got back in the car and drove back to the hotel.

It was now eleven o'clock and the couple was in their motel room. Sam had brought some champagne to celebrate their new freedom. They toasted.

"Look! It's a full moon," exclaimed Sylvia, pointing out the window and looking at the sky.

Sam stopped drinking, put the glass down and walked over to the window to look. "Hmm. Beautiful." Sylvia put two tranquillizers in his drink while he gazed up in the sky. After he finished his drink, they were in bed in ten minutes.

A few minutes later, Sam was out cold, sleeping. Sylvia left the room to get the dagger from Lucy who was parked in a hidden spot, about two hundred yards from the motel. She came back to the room quickly and stabbed Sam in the heart a few times. Then she put the dagger in Sam's luggage and walked out of the room with his luggage to Lucy's car. They drove into the motel parking lot, and after double-checking to make sure no one was looking, went into the room. They wrapped Sam up in a sheet that Lucy had brought, and, with great effort, picked him up and put him in the trunk. Sylvia double-checked to make sure no traces of blood were found in the bed, on the carpet, or on the pavement outside, and then got in the passenger's side of Lucy's car. They drove to the small lake where Calvin was silently resting. After checking thoroughly to see that no one was around, they dragged Sam out of the trunk. When they got to the end of the pier, they picked Sam up at both ends, ready to launch him into the water. "One, two, three!!" they exclaimed, as they threw the corpse into the water to join the other man of infidelity. The women sped off to go back to their homes.

"Well, we did it. We did it!" exclaimed Sylvia.

Lucy, the driver, gave a sigh.

"You know what the hardest part was?" Sylvia asked. "It was finding a way to put the tranquillizers into Sam's champagne without him noticing."

"Oh, the drink was champagne?" asked Lucy.

"Fortunately Sam brought champagne with him. Remember, the plan was to have us eat at the cafe *after* throwing in Calvin. That way I could put the tranquillizers in his coffee or whatever. But he just had to eat beforehand. Had he not brought the champagne, I don't know what I would have done. There was a full moon, and so I told Sam about it and while he was looking into the sky I dropped them into his drink."

"How many?" Lucy asked blandly.

"Two. That was plenty. He was out like a light in minutes. And everything about the motel was perfect. Having a room right off of the parking lot. And the few people that were at the motel must have been asleep. And Sam had filled me in with all of the details to the letter, so it was easy to inform you of everything. But wouldn't he have the smarts to figure out that the police would get suspicious of me if I just disappeared from town the day after Calvin's murder? Guess not."

Lucy just nodded.

"O.K., now Lucy, you know what happens next, don't you?" Sylvia continued. "Let's review. You drive me home. Then you drive to your home. You bury the dagger. Then at seven in the morning you call the police and tell them your husband hasn't come home and you've been up all night."

Lucy didn't respond, but started driving up in to the mountains near some steep cliffs.

Sylvia had withdrawn all the money from Calvin's bank accounts that afternoon. They had joint accounts, so it was easy. She had gotten all of Sam's money from his luggage at the motel after she knifed him. Sam had been coerced by Sylvia into withdrawing his thousands from the bank because it was going to be useless there. Sam believed they were going to Las Vegas to get married and spend the rest of their lives together under different names. She and Lucy were to split all the money, fifty-fifty. And when their husbands would eventually be pronounced dead after a few weeks because their bodies could not be found, they would collect life insurance from it. No one in town, including the police, was aware that Sylvia and Lucy knew each other, so no one would get the connection.

"We agreed a fifty-fifty split when we get the life insurance checks, right?" asked Sylvia.

"It won't matter," said Lucy, dully.

"What do you mean it won't matter? My, you're acting strange. You should be bouncing up and down with glee. What gives?"

"I'm going to commit suicide," Lucy said calmly. "This was one thing about this escapade that I kept from telling you, until now."

Sylvia looked at Lucy in shock. "I don't believe you. How can you do that? You're free from your husband who was going to divorce you. You have half of all this money. And you did a beautiful job in helping me get rid of our husbands."

"That was my final goal before I left this horrible world," said Lucy. "To help kill the people whom I despised the most. My husband who was messing around with you, and your husband that had the gall to mess around with me."

"What?"

"Now, being vindicated, I can rest in peace."

"You're crazy," Sylvia exclaimed. "Now you can begin to live. Look at the money you have now, off of both Sam and Calvin."

"Money doesn't bring happiness."

"Yes it does!"

"No. If it did, I would have chosen my other alternative. I would have gotten a gun and killed you right now, and taken the bags of money totally for myself. But it's not worth it. Life has too many disappointments to continue living. And you disappointed me too, Sylvia. I'm sure you encouraged Sam to stalk after you. It takes two to tango, as they say. I think you liked him and you'd still be with him, except you'd rather get half of his thousands. So I'll be killing you as well, along with myself."

Sylvia then realized Lucy was about to drive off the cliff. Her face went white with fear. "Lucy!"

"My plan worked perfectly. It was the only way I could get all three of you."

"Lucy. LUCY!"

Sylvia quickly opened the door on the passenger side to escape, but Lucy, with her right hand, grabbed Sylvia's arm to prevent her from escaping, and with her left hand turned the steering wheel so that the car drove off the cliff and plummeted down the embankment. The car tumbled over twice and landed on its top when it reached the bottom about two hundred feet below the road.

The owner of the motel, Charles, along with the custodian, Rich, had been driving behind Lucy's car. Charles, in his dark motel room, had seen Sylvia and Lucy through the blinds carry something about six feet long with a sheet over it from a motel room to the trunk of a car. At first, Charles thought it was a long piece of furniture, but couldn't recall a piece of furniture with that dimension in any of his motel rooms. He then saw them drive on the dirt road that led basically to nowhere, he thought, except to a coffee plantation. Getting suspicious, he immediately had Rich call the police and asked him to watch the motel while he got dressed to get in his truck and follow the ladies. By the time he got dressed and was in the truck ready to leave, he saw the same car come back from the dirt road, pass the motel, and head on up the road that led to the mountains. Charles motioned for Rich, who had already notified the police, to get in the truck with him in case he needed more help.

They saw the car go off the cliff. They stopped their truck on the side of the road and got out quickly with their flashlights. They were able to slide down the side of the cliff without any danger because the angle was not that steep. The full moon and their flashlights aided their progress. When the men got to the bottom, they noticed the two women were dead. The keys were still in the ignition. Charles took out the keys and opened the trunk. There was no corpse to be found. In looking inside the car they saw some luggage with a dagger inside, and two bags full of money. Charles took the bags and began counting the money as Rich watched him count while licking his lips.

"Well, there's fifteen thousand in this one bag. And there's another ten thousand in this one," stated Charles.

"Whoa, we hit it big," said Rich excitedly.

"Let's get back up to the truck." Charles never showed much emotion but lived a quiet, serene life. He also seemed to be in a pleasant mood regardless of the circumstances. "We need to drive back to the motel because the police will arrive soon if they haven't already, and keep this money safe. We can only tell the police what we know. Nothing more."

They began to climb the side of the cliff.

"Do you think it's safe to tell the police they drove off the cliff? Won't they suspect us of something?" asked Rich.

"Not when we give them all this money we found. We're not going to keep it," said Charles calmly. "They'll know we're honest."

Rich stopped his climbing and looked at Charles with incredulity. He continued staring as Charles continued climbing.

"You mean we're not going to keep this?" Rich asked.

"It's not ours. Perhaps this money belongs to the deceased's family. Perhaps they have a will." He looked at Rich sternly, and then continued going up the last part of the cliff but spoke loud enough for Rich to hear. "I don't take what doesn't belong to me. I learn to be happy with what I have, and what I earn."

Rich stood motionless, staring with disgust at Charles who continued up the slope, until the blackness of the night, even with the full moon, removed him from his sight.

❦   ❦   ❦

Over the next several days, Charles cooperated with the police and the crime detectives in the attempt to sort everything out. He had told them what he saw from his dark motel room. The bodies of Sylvia and Lucy were easily identified. The police knew of the apparent murder of Calvin, based on what Sylvia had told them, and what Thelma told them with her witnessing the phone call. They also knew that Sam was missing from the auto shop and no one could locate him. So both husbands of the two women were nowhere to be found. The detectives saw that all the money in the bank accounts of Sam and Calvin was withdrawn the same day that their wives drove over the cliff. It was virtually the same amount that Russell gave to the police, who, in turn, put in a safe for the time being. It was obvious to see that there was foul play. The women did not draw up any will, but Sam and Calvin did. Their relatives were anxious to receive the inheritance money that Charles found in the car, and also the life insurance payments. But the bodies of the two men needed to be found. So they posted a reward of thousands for anyone who could help in leading to the whereabouts of the supposed corpses and the details of their alleged deaths. Charles had always believed that the man he saw with Sylvia at his cafe on that fateful night was, indeed, Sam Downs, based on the pictures of him the relatives produced. But he couldn't prove anything, because the woman Sam was with signed the register with a name no one knew, and the room was paid with cash. Because of the reward offered, Charles, along with detectives, would continue to spend much time looking in areas around the half-mile dirt road driven by the women who apparently buried a body—or two. They surveyed all the way to the end of the road where the coffee plantation was, trying to find a hidden grave, and found nothing.

Then one day, Charles decided to go beyond the end of the dirt road and hike up a small hill. To his surprise he saw a small, hidden lake with a short pier. At the end of the pier, he saw a toupee floating around. He had to jump in the water to grab it. The lake was dragged and the detectives found both men. Charles used half of his reward money for a much-deserved lengthy vacation to Europe, and used the other half to pay his nephew's college expenses.

Medicine

I remember that the hospital looked plain, cold, and hard, and the nurses mirrored my impression of the building. Of course, hospitals were not built to impress people with architectural creativity, but to be a source for healing—and not necessarily of the conventional kind. As the nurses motioned to the choir and me what room to enter, they looked like robots—straight faces, unemotional and unfeeling.

Everyone including myself and the director of the choir seemed rather quiet on the bus ride from the church this Sunday afternoon. It was a twenty-six mile trip one way. I was the piano accompanist for the choir and, frankly, would have rather stayed home and watched NBA basketball on television, sinking down into my newly-bought reclining chair. But we came for a worthy cause. A custodian for our church, Harold, had accidentally fallen fifty feet from the ceiling of our gym as he was putting in the sound system for the children's musical. He landed on his back and became paralyzed. Harold had been in the hospital for four weeks, we knew he was in a wheel chair and, understandably, deeply depressed. The church choir had come to sing a few hymns to Harold, console him, and hopefully lift his spirits. No one knew if he would ever walk again.

"Show us where the piano is please," said Roger the director, to the nurses. The choir remained in a room while Roger and I followed a couple of nurses down the hall.

"This is . . . all we have," said one nurse. I didn't expect much of a piano, and it was worse than what I imagined even before playing it. The ivory was off half of the keys, some keys were missing, and the frame was wobbly. I played a couple of chords and estimated the last tuning to have been before the civil war. Roger obviously did not check ahead of time to see that this facility had a decent instrument, and I was angry. We could have brought an electronic piano from the church.

"I know it isn't much," said the nurse, forcing a smile. "We did have another piano as well, but discarded it—it was worse than this one."

Roger was silent, then said blandly, "Let's wheel it on in," and started pushing the piano to our room. I was hoping the piano would collapse before reaching its destination so I could simply sing with the choir, but it arrived in one piece. Before Harold arrived, we rehearsed a verse and everyone laughed in hearing the piano, while I tried to contain my frustration.

"They discarded a piano that was worse than this one," said Roger who was laughing, and everyone else joined in the merriment. It wasn't like playing a guitar or violin where I could control the intonation.

They wheeled in Harold who was indeed surprised to see his own church choir come to sing for him. He wouldn't speak. Yet his face spoke for him. After he showed his surprised look, his depressed look took over. Harold was in his early thirties as I, the prime of life.

Roger told Harold what was going to be sung and waited for some sign of pleasantness in Harold's face, but it wouldn't come. The choir, about fifteen in number, became uneasy but got their music out.

Roger looked over at me. "O.K. Larry, let's start with 'Nearer My God to Thee'." I started playing the intro from the hymnbook, and the choir changed from solemnity to quiet laughter as they wondered if they would be able to stay on pitch with the piano.

After a couple of verses, Roger said, "Doesn't Larry play out of tune?" And the choir laughed. Harold did not. He remained sitting motionless in his wheel chair, eyes staring straight ahead.

Roger chose a couple of hymns that were livelier. The choir snickered during each piano introduction. The choir sang, Roger directed, I played. There was still no response from Harold. So it was time for another tasteless joke from Roger.

"I wish you could play a hymn in the same key from beginning to end, Larry," Roger bellowed. The choir laughed, and even the straight-faced nurses cracked some smiles. Harold looked at Roger, then looked at the choir, then looked at me. But his expression remained motionless.

I was tempted to shout, "It's not my fault that no one took the time in preparation to see that this place had a decent instrument. Go ahead without me. Try it without me!" But I decided to contain myself. Even if the piano *was* out of tune, they needed to get their pitches.

Roger chose one more hymn after the laughter settled down. I saw Harold scowl out of the corner of my eye. Just one more hymn and all of this will be over, I thought. Again I started the introduction. Again the same snickering until they began to sing the verse.

After the hymn, Roger looked at Harold who had not shown one glimmer of hope or satisfaction. Roger tried to remain optimistic, looked intently at Harold and said, "I hope you have enjoyed our singing and trust that you have been inspired by the words of these hymns." Harold continued to have a stern face. "We're very sorry about the piano," Roger continued. "It couldn't be helped."

"You don't need to apologize for the piano," Harold said abruptly. The fact that a response came from Harold shocked everybody. Then he looked at the piano. "The piano's condition is very similar to mine. It's broken down, it needs repair, it's handicapped. You people may laugh at the piano, but I don't appreciate that kind of laughter. But I do appreciate Larry." He looked right at me. "You knew the piano wasn't very good to play on but you went ahead and performed anyway because you felt it had some use. I hope people can see beyond my handicap to realize I can still be of some use to the world."

I saw Harold smile a little, and, for the first time, his face had a glimmer of hope as he looked at me. "You gave me a much needed shot in the arm, Larry. Thanks for coming." There was a sense of fulfillment in his face. He motioned for the nurses to wheel him back to his room, and ignored Roger and the choir as he exited, leaving them in stony silence.

It was one of my most memorable days as an accompanist. I remember leaving the room while Roger and the choir had their heads bowed. Then I called a relative who came and took me home, while the choir and director left on the bus.

Mountains

Driving down from Bishop on the 395 for the nth time caused Dollie Eddy to go into a deep sleep when they were approaching Lone Pine. Her newest husband, Sam Kyles, was behind the wheel, and the cool air conditioner would always cause Dollie to drowse as they drove through the desert.

Sam was her fourth husband. She was thirty-five and one of the country's premier actresses. She had just finished shooting a film in Hollywood that took three months of hard work, and then had gone to Bishop for a week's vacation after marrying Sam. She loved the desert town and thought it would be a good place to honeymoon instead of the glamorous places like Waikiki, Rome, or Paris.

Sam slowed to a stop and turned off the air conditioner. The lack of air and stopping after driving for so long woke up Dollie.

"What are you doing?" she said, in a cranky manner.

"I'm hungry. I want to get a quick bite."

"Well, I'm not. Let's keep going. I want to get back to L.A. before sunset."

"Why?"

"Because I want to."

"But . . . we're going to have to stop eventually anyway to eat between here and L.A. It's about a five hour drive and. . . ."

"Listen, I don't want to stop here, O.K.?" she interrupted, beginning to shout. "I'm not hungry. I was comfortable sleeping with the air on. Why did you turn it off for? Don't just think of yourself." She turned it back on, grunted, and leaned back and closed her eyes again after delivering a big sigh.

Sam just sat there looking at her for a few seconds and then turned on the ignition while shaking his head. His stomach growled, while he thought of Dollie's first three husbands.

A minute later when Dollie found out she couldn't sleep, she looked out the car window.

"There's Mt. Whitney," she said, pointing to a mountain.

"Oh. So what?"

"Well, it's the tallest mountain in the continental United States. Over fourteen thousand feet above sea level, I think," she said, looking at what she thought was the peak because it appeared to be the highest mountain of that range.

"How high are we here in Lone Pine?" asked Sam.

"Oh, about four thousand, I guess," she said.

Sam's stomach growled some more.

"I am so hungry," he said. "Are you sure we can't stop. . . ."

"No! I want to get home. Don't mention it again."

Sam had been married to her for seven days. He had gotten annoyed with her each day about something, but this was the ultimate in frustration.

A few miles south of Lone Pine, Dollie got excited.

"Oh! A palm reader! Let's stop!" she exclaimed.

"What?"

"The sign. See it? It says *palm reader*. Palm reading has always fascinated me. Stop the car."

"But . . . I thought you wanted to get home."

"I want to see the palm reader," Dollie said assertively, slapping the dashboard. "Don't argue."

Sam stopped the car, put it in reverse, and drove backwards some two hundred feet on the sand next to the pavement of the road, the same direction he felt his relationship was going with Dollie.

"Maybe I can find something to eat around here while that idiot fools with your hand," he said.

"No. You're coming with me," she said, grabbing his hand, pulling him into the little hut after her.

The hut had two small rooms—a waiting room separated by a curtain from the other room where the palm reader did her work. The palmist was busy with someone else, so Sam and Dollie were told to wait on the bench by a teenage girl, coated with makeup.

"Isn't this exciting?" Dollie asked exuberantly to Sam.

Sam's stomach growled.

Within five minutes, they were called in.

"I think I'll wait out here," said Sam.

"Oh, come on!" shouted Dollie to her husband, grabbing him by the arm and pulling him into the next room with her. "Don't be so selfish!"

They both sat down with the palmist who immediately recognized her new customer as the world famous Dollie Eddy, and was stunned by the fiery attitude she had toward the man she was with. After getting herself back together over the thought of examining a person so well-known, she examined Dollie's hand closely, then spoke.

"You will find a very special man in the desert some day. You will marry this man."

"Gee, I hope he doesn't have a strong appetite," Sam inserted.

"You will remain a very successful actress," the palmist continued, "and continue in great wealth, but your life will strangely remain unfulfilled. You will have longings for ultimate fulfillment that will not be met."

"I've already met my man in the desert and I just married him a week ago," said Dollie, poking her finger in Sam's ribs.

"No. This is in the future," said the palmist. "You will meet a man in the future and he will be someone who lives in the desert."

"Come on, let's go," said Sam, uneasily.

"Shut up, will you!" screamed Dollie. The she looked at the palmist. "I think you're two weeks behind. Sam here is from the desert and I married him last week. I do not intend on ever marrying again. Ever."

"You will, in the future, marry someone who lives in the desert, and you will have sons."

"Sons? Really? How many?"

"I can't tell you."

Sam's stomach growled again.

"Well, tell me about them," said Dollie, very amused, almost laughing, but deeply curious.

"I can't. All I can tell you is that you will have sons." The palmist then looked at Sam.

"Come on, let's go," he said, standing up.

Dollie stood up after some deep thinking, and paid the fee. They left and got in the car.

After watching them leave, the palmist said to the teenage girl who was her understudy, "If you see someone screaming in public at those that are supposed to be close to them, you can always tell them they will have an unfulfilled life, and usually you'll be right." They both snickered.

Sam finally got a meal a couple of hours later when Dollie felt hungry and demanded that Sam immediately stop the car so they could go to the nearest cafe.

Three days later a few of Hollywood's dignitaries gave Dollie and Sam a party at a Beverly Hills mansion. Dollie liked parties.

It got her mind off of some of the depressing things of life and helped her to concentrate on the things she thrived on: other people who adored her, and plenty of attention. Sam, who was a screenwriter, enjoyed parties too but for a different reason. It gave him an excuse to get away from the typewriter. He was a hard worker, and it was said around Hollywood that he spent more time with the typewriter than any other screenwriter. There was a rumor he went to bed with it if he was on a creative binge. If his fellow screenwriters were to see him dead, the thought of burying the typewriter with him would be considered.

Everyone at the party knew that this was a crucial marriage for Dollie. She had always wanted a lifelong companion, a husband that would stay with her and love her, and children she could raise. She loved the glamour of the Hollywood life, the movies, the stardom, the popularity, the fan mail, the spotlights, the attention, the wealth, but it was not enough to give her the happiness she wanted. Dollie wanted to be permanently married, and wanted to know that this husband truly loved her and would stay loyal regardless of her shortcomings. She knew Sam was her man, and had already tested him out before they got married. Dollie was purposefully mean and rigid to see how he would react. He remained calm and stable in his attitude, and would treat her always the same. Her previous three marriages had lasted only two years each and she made life miserable for each man. One had committed suicide after Dollie refused to divorce without suing. The other two simply could not stand her condescension and divorced, finding someone else quickly thereafter. Those that new Dollie, the directors, the producers, film editors, anyone who worked with her, were hopeful this marriage would give her the true happiness she always wanted. Their hope was that a good marriage would make it easier to work with her, as Dollie's work habits were anything but congenial.

The master of ceremonies gave them a toast to launch the party, and then the people mingled and danced. While she was dancing with Sam, Dollie noticed her younger sister and only sibling, Marian, sitting on the other side of the room. She was alone but looked content, sipping some champagne.

Dollie stopped dancing and motioned for Sam to come with her and meet her sister. She hadn't seen her in almost a year.

Marian was twenty-eight and happily single. She had not even tried to compete with her older sister. In high school, Dollie was more attractive and more popular, getting all of the leads in the school plays. She also got higher grades. But Marian was self-sufficient and happy, and didn't need others to boost her ego. She lived in a two-story apartment with her girlfriend, and was an account coordinator for an ice cream product at an ad agency. Marian didn't make a lot of money, but enough to keep her above water, and that was enough to keep her satisfied. Dollie needed glamour, excitement, and wealth to survive. Marian did not. And somehow, it was Dollie that respected Marian who could find a way to be satisfied with what appeared to be a normal, humdrum existence. Dollie couldn't live an average lifestyle, but realized that Marian looked to other things for fulfillment.

"Why are you sitting here all alone like a wallflower?" Dollie asked her, smiling.

Marian stood up, smiled and said, "I'm all right. I'll survive, believe me. The friends I was talking to left for some reason or another."

"This is my husband, Sam. A sober Sam. You better meet him quick before the party goes too long."

Marian extended her arm to shake.

"Hello Marian," said Sam as he shook hands.

"I saw your picture in the paper with Dollie," said Marian. "You know, of the wedding." It had been a simple private wedding, with a minister and photographer. None of the family attended.

"Oh yes," said Sam. "Front page coverage. I finally did something that got on the front page. None of the scripts made it."

"Oh darling, don't beat yourself over the head with a broomstick," Dollie said in a whining tone of voice. "Look how the front page coverage I've gotten in my career has done little for my enjoyment of life."

Marian's expression changed to a cold one, and Sam cleared his throat.

"I . . . I see some of my colleagues have just arrived," said Sam as he looked at the entrance. "Why don't we go over and talk to them?"

"You go ahead," said Dollie. "I want to talk to Marian."

Sam left.

"I hate it when he tells me what I should do," said Dollie, unreasonably.

Marian looked at Dollie strangely. She was about to speak when Dollie noticed a man coming toward Marian.

"Hello," said Dollie to him.

"I moved my car so I can be sure to get out when I leave," said the man to Marian.

"Doug, this is . . ." started Marian.

"Ah, Dollie Eddy," said Doug. "Glad to meet you. Where did your husband run off to?"

Dollie didn't answer. "I'll converse with you later, Marian. We haven't seen each other in a year. We have some catching up to do."

"Yes, we do."

Dollie left quickly, leaving Doug alone with Marian.

"Strange woman," he said.

"She's not strange," Marian said, starting to smile, looking at her sister walk away.

"Marvelous actress. She can play any role," said Doug. "But I hear she's a bitch to work with. The directors when deciding whether to choose Dollie for a part always wonder whether her tremendous talent is worth putting up with her irascible nature. What do you think?"

"She's my sister. I'm not going to say anything bad about her."

Three months later, Dollie and Sam needed to get away from the big city for a week so they were up in Bishop again. Dollie continued to hate the way she acted, but seemed resigned to the fact it was the only way for her to be, and couldn't be escaped.

Sam was sitting in the living room of their hotel suite at eleven o'clock at night. She was sitting across from him. After looking at the clock, she got up slowly and began walking towards the bedroom. He knew it meant she was through for the day and there would be no involvement with him the rest of the night. Otherwise she would have walked straight toward him and started her love play.

"I'm lonely," he said.

She stopped walking and looked at him. She didn't say anything and then turned and walked into the bedroom. The light was out in two minutes. He got up five minutes later and opened the door and heard her snoring softly.

Sam went back to his chair in the living room and sat down. Yes, he was very lonely. He didn't have his typewriter. It would usually keep him company but he had to leave it at home in Beverly Hills, otherwise it wouldn't be a vacation. He wanted some excitement, so he got up and drove to a night club just a block down on the main drag. He watched people walk in to the club while sitting in his car in the adjacent parking lot. There were very few couples or groups. Virtually everyone was going in alone. Sam got out of the car and went inside. He was thankful, at this particular time, that he was not world famous like his wife. He didn't want to be bothered by autographs and everyone looking at him.

He sat at a table away from the bar and relaxed, surveying everyone within eyeshot. Ah, a screenwriter's dream. To critique other people, look in their faces, and try to figure out what they are thinking, where they immediately came from, and where they will be going when they leave the club. He loved to survey two people talking to each other, what they might be saying based on the expression of their faces, whether they really like the person being spoken to, checking out their body language, trying to figure out what their passions are. Sam was hoping these people could give him a springboard to a plot that could start a new screenplay. But nothing triggered, as most of these people looked as lonely as he was. They all looked as if they were waiting for something to happen, even though they had different faces and different expressions.

A waitress came to him and he ordered a beer. When he got the drink, he walked around and looked at the people closely without being a snoop. He eyed some women, and some women eyed him, but the glances weren't long. By the time Sam sat down again he had finished his drink.

He went back in his car and watched the people walk in and walk out of the club. Sam drove a block to the hotel, and was now lonelier than when he left his living room. In walking to his suite, it gave him time to reflect on the weeks of his marriage to Dollie.

Sam walked into his suite, changed clothes, and immediately went to bed. Dollie was asleep but Sam knew she awoke when he grabbed the covers. He turned over on his side with his back to her. A few weeks ago he had felt the same loneliness in bed, and then she snuggled next to him and gave him a bear hug from the back which remained the entire evening. He was hoping the same would happen tonight and she would take the initiative. Sam wanted to feel the vibrations of her warm body, and his loneliness would be gone.

He was certain Dollie knew he was waiting for her, but she never came close. Sam longed for her a few more minutes before he fell asleep.

Within a few months, Marian was married to Doug, the man Dollie saw very briefly at the party in their Beverly Hills mansion. Marian had actually known him for years, and he was starting to make a name for himself in Hollywood as a fine film editor. The wedding was in a church, and a much bigger wedding than the ones Dollie had participated in for herself. She was the maid-of-honor and felt as out of place as an animal in the wrong cage at a zoo. But if she didn't participate, many of the Hollywood dignitaries who were at the wedding because of Doug would wonder why. She didn't want them to know her unhappiness of the whole affair. Her younger sister was truly happy, and this made her jealous. Dollie would never let anyone know it, not in a million years.

At the reception, a number of celebrities and newspaper reporters were on hand, and talked more about Dollie than the bride. There was a shade of resentment from the Hollywood crowd over Marian's fulfillment in life without being part of the elite.

"Are you going to throw your bouquet, my darling?" Doug asked.

"Not yet. I still haven't greeted all the guests yet," Marian said glowingly. "Where is Sam, by the way? I haven't seen him. Dollie is not with him."

"That is not too surprising. I'm sure she is keeping herself busy with reporters. Oh . . . there he is. Talking to Russ Huff, a director. He's trying to score some points."

"Well I hope he succeeds. Have you worked with Russ?"

"Not yet. He's too selective when it comes to film editors. If he likes an editor on a prior film, he tries to keep the same guy for the future. Well, hello, Tony."

"Lucky fellow, Doug," said Tony, shaking hands. "How long have you two known each other?"

"Mm, five years," said Marian.

"Beautiful wedding. I don't know why Dollie looked so serious coming down the aisle, though. Could it be she was . . . dare I say it, nervous?" Tony asked.

"Dollie? Nervous?" Marian immediately chimed in. "She hasn't a nervous bone in her body."

"I'm sure it was very meaningful for her to be in her sister's wedding," Doug affirmed. "She was doing something different. Her weddings have always been very private, you know, in front of a handful of people with a Justice of the Peace."

"Oh, there are the Clendons," Marian said excitedly, and intentionally changing the subject. "I'll need to talk to her about something."

"Go ahead," urged Doug. Marian walked over to them.

"The difference is striking," said Tony to Doug after Marian left.

"What do you mean?" asked Doug.

"Dollie and Marian."

"Oh, I know. Everyone knows. She's been in her sister's shadow for years, and doesn't care. She's actually a phenomenal woman. A nice, quiet, charming young lady."

"Well, best wishes to you," said Tony to Doug, taking a drink from a woman who obviously wanted to converse. "Got to go."

Dollie stayed in her marriage with Sam for two years, her quota. It ended quickly when she lost her temper after having one too many drinks and threw an ashtray at his face when he refused to change a channel to Dollie's favorite program. A shouting match ensued and Sam walked out. He filed the divorce papers at the urging of his screenwriter friends, and when they separated, Sam felt the same freedom one would feel leaving the inside of a cage with a mountain lion.

Fifteen years after Marian's wedding, Dollie, and her new husband Charles, were driving south on the 395 from Lake Tahoe where they honeymooned. They had already passed Bishop and were nearing Lone Pine.

Charles was driving the car. He was her seventh husband. Dollie was now fifty and as well-known a star as could be found. She was wealthier, received more print, and was as unfulfilled as ever. The more she got, the more she wanted.

Dollie had not yet met a husband in the desert as the palmist had predicted. She met Charles in the mountains three months previous, and he had two teenage sons from a prior marriage, making them her step sons. So Dollie felt the palmist was at least half-right in the prediction regarding her sons.

Marian had four children now and continued to be happily married to Doug, who continued his success as a film editor, being nominated twice for an Oscar and attaining national attention. After the children came, she left the ad agency business to be a stay-at-home mom, loving every minute of it, with the prospect of returning to her career after the kids grew older. When the sisters would get together, Dollie would always get an ear full from Marian about the euphoria of being a mother and raising a family. This was something Dollie never looked forward to, and inwardly despised her sister. She would remain as aloof from Marian as possible, enjoying instead the idolizing crowd of fans that would follow her around. She was sensitive about the fact she didn't have children, and it was difficult for her to be a good aunt. It was difficult to give the nieces and nephews presents for their birthdays, when she wished those children were her own.

As they were approaching Lone Pine, Dollie remembered a former conversation she had with another fellow at this precise spot. She immediately turned her head and looked at the mountain range west of her.

"That's Mt. Whitney," she said, pointing to a peak. "Tallest mountain in America, except for the ones in Alaska."

"No, it's not," said Charles, smoking a cigarette. "That's Lone Pine Peak."

Dollie turned her head to Charles in disgust. "What do you mean? I've been driving along this road a number of times. I know which mountain is which, and I've seen that mountain range hundreds of times."

"I'm sure you've driven on this road many times and for many years, knowing how much you like the desert and Bishop," he said calmly, exhaling some smoke. "The mountain you pointed to looks the tallest from our vantage point because it's closer to us and looks more prominent." Charles stopped the car on the side of the road. "Mt. Whitney is over there." He pointed to a peak that was to the right, and back further. "Fourteen thousand four hundred and ninety-six feet above sea level, give or take a few inches here or there. It doesn't look as tall because we are farther away from it. And it doesn't look so prominent, like Lone Pine Peak. It's just back there minding its business in the background, as if it doesn't care whether people notice it or not."

Dollie was quiet for a few seconds, and then spoke. "I'm going to ask a gas station attendant or somebody to make sure."

"Dollie! What difference does it make? What difference in the world does it make? Why, for goodness sake?"

"Drive up to the next gas station," Dollie ordered.

Charles complied, as he had done during the entire honeymoon. He hadn't been hardened yet.

They stopped at a gas station, and Dollie got out almost before the car came to a complete stop.

"Dollie Eddy!" exclaimed the gas station attendant. "Dollie Eddy. Boy, I never thought a movie star like you would ever come into *my* gas station." He raced inside to get a pad so he could get her autograph. She saw the attention coming her way from the other customers at the station, and this unnerved her. A question answered was all she wanted at this point.

The attendant came out with a notepad and pencil.

"I don't want to give my autograph," Dollie tried to say calmly. "I want a question answered. Where is Mt. Whitney?"

"Mt. Whitney. Let's see, it's that peak right . . . right there." He stood right next to her so she could get his point of view and pointed to the peak Charles had pointed.

"I always thought it was *that* one," said Dollie, rather sheepishly, pointed to another one.

"No, that's . . . that's Lone Pine Peak, I believe. That's about thirteen thousand feet. It kind of looks taller than the others, don't it? That's because it's closer to us, I guess. Say do you want some gas?"

"No thank you," she said, and immediately got back in the car.

They drove off.

"All right, I'm convinced," she said.

Charles, the philosopher, started his ramble. "You know, mountains are sort of like people." He stopped and contemplated what he just said, and then continued. "There are some people that are more prominent and closer to the general public but that doesn't make them the highest. You know what I mean? Then there are some others who aren't as prominent and are kind of quiet and in the background, but in reality are taller. . . ." Charles stopped and knew he had blown it. He wished he could rewind the tape and draw all the words back. Seeing Dollie's face, he knew she was hurt.

Within a minute, Dollie's face was covered with tears. She tried to remember the last time she cried. It must have been her teenage years, decades ago. She never cried at funerals, or watching sad movies. She never had any movie roles that involved crying. Twice as an adult, she was with a small group of ladies that were all weeping but her.

As they were driving out of Lone Pine, he said, "I shouldn't have said . . . I shouldn't have said that."

"Yes, you should have," she said in a voice that was shaking and barely audible. "I'm being cleansed."

"You're being . . . what? I'm sure I don't understand."

Charles then said something else, but it couldn't be heard because of the loudness of a truck coming in the opposite direction.

A minute later, he said, "Let's stop the car and walk around a bit. Maybe you'll feel better." He slowed down and was about to drive off the road.

"No!" she begged, almost shouting. "Damn it, keep going, Charles!"

He drove up to the normal speed. Charles noticed Dollie immediately become calm again, as more tears began to flow from her eyes and down her cheeks.

"Charles, it's O.K.," she said meekly, tugging on his arm affectionately. "It feels so good to cry again. I'm being cleansed. Thank you."

Dollie forced a smile as more tears came. Charles offered his handkerchief but she refused it. Dollie wanted more tears to come and didn't want them dried. Her face expressed sorrow, peace, hope, optimism.

Charles looked at her sympathetically, and then focused on the road. He shook his head in bewilderment as he threw his cigarette out the window.

SPEECH!

For an office job, the physical surroundings were standard, and the social surroundings were normal. The building, located in Los Angeles, was twenty-five stories, with the Gellem and Bates Advertising Agency taking up the fifth through the eighth floors. The social atmosphere always contained rumors, and sometimes it contained more false than true, which was not unusual for an office job. Rumors had to be circulating in order to keep life interesting at the agency. Otherwise, all you had to concentrate on was your work for seven and a half hours, daily. There had to be gossip and stories circulating to make people really want to come to work. It made your actual work easier. And as long as there were about two hundred people working together, as was the case at Gellem and Bates, it was inevitable that rumors would fly around.

There was the rumor that because Linda Carnes had changed her address to be the same as Bill Davidley two weeks after she became employed, it must mean she was having an affair with Bill in the same apartment complex. Everybody but Linda and Bill had heard this story that was circulating in the media department. All eyes were on them when they came to work and when they left. There was another story circulating that Sam Samuelson's marriage was on the decline when he was seen with three different women at lunch within five days. Everybody knew he wasn't talking business. Some eavesdroppers heard some bits and pieces of the conversations.

Then there was the time when the agency lost a ten million dollar account. There would be layoffs, approximately ten from each of the major departments. The massive layoff was to occur on a Friday, and each employee was checking out how their supervisor was treating them that week. Did the supervisor's silence mean he didn't want to talk to the employee that was about to be laid off, or was it that he was still thinking about what to do. Or if the boss was exceptionally nice to an employee, then that person really had to worry. It was to show that if the ax came down on Friday it was nothing personal, and to hope the employee would have a good last impression of him. The media director that week had a list of the ten people that would lose their jobs, and it either got misplaced or stolen. Everybody in the media department knew it was gone and probably stolen, and if stolen, the robber was the only person who knew where it was. Whenever someone went to another person's desk to borrow a pen or paper clip from a drawer, they would secretly look to see if that person had the list in that drawer. The list was never found, and it didn't matter. The ten on the list were laid off on Friday and that was that. The media director, starting at ten o'clock, went around to the different offices to inform the individuals about the cutback in the budget and they would have to go. It was all done in about fifteen minutes. The entire department was in stony silence as the director made his rounds from office to office. After he finished and the rest of the troops counted ten people packing up and moving out, there was a general sigh of relief, and at lunch time it seemed everyone went out and got drunk in celebration so that no one was much good for anything the rest of the afternoon.

Just a few days before the agency's annual Holiday party, the newest topic on everyone's mind was who would be announced as the new Vice-President. The latest associate media director had resigned a month previous, and there were two supervisors that were next in line to receive a promotion to the vacated position. The position had to be filled, and there were only two young men that could meet the qualifications. One was Barry Lord, who had been with the agency for five years and had worked his way up from being a media assistant. He was a strong leader, aggressive, an extrovert. But he was impulsive, occasionally offended people, and was hesitant to apologize. The other was Brad Davis, who was somewhat the opposite of Barry. He was on the quiet side, introverted, and extremely bright. He lacked the leadership ability that Barry had, but was very studious, able to listen, and a team player. The media department was split down the middle as to who would be the best associate media director and earn the right to the title of Vice-President. A couple of media planners even laid bets on the matter. And anytime someone in the department had a reason for claiming one was better than another, someone else would point out the strength of the other fellow. The final decision was to be made by the media director, Chuck McDermott, but his decision could be influenced by the board of directors at the agency.

It was Wednesday, two days before the Holiday party when the promotions were announced. Brad and Barry happened to cross paths in the restroom. There was silence for a few seconds as each one could not think of something to say while they each were standing in front of the urinal. Finally Barry spoke.

"Have you gotten any clues from Chuck?"

"None."

"I haven't either. I just hope the whole thing gets over with on Friday," said Barry, wearily.

"It will. If not I'll let you have the promotion. I don't like this waiting game. I haven't lost a wink of sleep over it though."

"Really? I've been getting only four hours of sleep a night. Hey, that's bad for me. I'm worrying about it more than you. In advertising, the one who worries more usually loses."

Brad laughed. "There you go again, analyzing every cotton-pickin' thing. If you're in a meeting with a client and he has one of his buttons in the middle of his shirt unbuttoned, you'll think it means something."

"Actually, it does," Barry responded quickly. "It means he either has poor eyesight and needs to be sent his monthly bill with enlarged letters so we can be paid promptly, or it means he doesn't believe in looking in the mirror at himself because he knows he's perfect, has a swell-head, and so therefore is impossible to be persuaded on anything that isn't his idea in the first place. Those are the toughest clients of all."

"Sounds like you're going to have everything under control if you get V.P.," assured Brad, beginning to walk out.

"Well, the last few weeks I've been thinking how I would react in different situations with the clients," said Barry. "Being V.P. means the company has full confidence that that person can tactfully do the job in front of the client." Barry followed Brad out the door.

"That's a key word right there," Brad agreed. "Tact. Sometimes it means not saying anything. I'm not sure I would always know when to say something and when not to, or to what client. Sometimes they just want you to nod your head because they've already made up their minds."

"You've got to convince them of your idea before they've made up their minds," Barry said forcefully, as they walked to their mail slots. "Clients really aren't that smart. That's the reason they need an agency, and they know it. We need to do their thinking for them."

Brad just smiled.

"Well, you need to have the aggressive approach, you know," Barry said egotistically, then laughed at his own snobbery. "Set them straight."

"Sounds like you've made yourself ready," said Brad, looking at junk mail in his mail slot.

"I've got to be mentally ready if I land that title." Barry noticed a surprising nervous quiver in his voice.

"Just don't have a heart attack if they call your name this Friday, because then I'll have to take your place knowing I didn't get the vote." Brad walked to his office as Barry followed him inside.

"Don't tell me *you're* not nervous," Barry retorted, with his eyebrows raised.

"I'm not really," Brad said calmly. "If I don't get it, I still have my job here. The company has been good to me. I'm glad that Gellem promotes from within. Either of us two would be better than an outsider taking the position."

"If someone from the outside came in and got it, I'd quit. I would." Barry opened his mail and continued. "That would be a slap in the face to me and I wouldn't stand it. I've worked hard and I don't feel the company has been that good to me."

"What do you mean? You started out as a media assistant just a few years ago. They've treated you well."

"Well, here I go again, but, frankly, I deserved to get moved up. They knew I'd quit if they didn't promote me." Barry spoke softer. "You've got to use the scare tactic on ole Chuck to get anywhere in this media department. I even let him see my resume laying on my desk once just to let him know I was planning to leave. Two weeks later they moved me up from planner to senior planner."

Brad just smiled, while Barry shook his head and threw his junk mail away.

"You would have gotten the senior planner position anyway, wouldn't you?" asked Brad. "Wasn't it the time for your review?"

"Yeah, it was. I just wanted to make sure Chuck put me where I thought I belonged."

"Well, you're aggressive and I have to hand that to you," said Brad. "But hang loose. Hopefully we'll still be friends after Friday, won't we? Just take things as they come."

Brad sat down in his chair behind his desk, throwing away some mail and putting the rest of it in a couple of stacks.

"Is that your son, John?" asked Barry, pointing to the picture of Brad's two-year-old son that was on the desk. "He's grown since the last time I saw him."

"Yeah, they tend to do that."

"It's nice to have a family to go home to after a hard day of work. I just have my sofa and television," Barry scoffed.

"The choice is yours."

"That's why I take my job so seriously, I guess. I have nothing else to fall back on. Nothing else to go to if I fail at this."

"The choice is yours," Brad said again.

"Yes. You're right. Well, I guess I need to get to my desk and work on that media plan some more. Chuck wants to see it at four. See you."

"Try to concentrate," said Brad as Barry left the room.

That evening the media department of Gellem had a party at a home of one of the employees. The living room was totally crowded, and there was loud music in the background. There were cookies, punch, and beer. People were gathered together in small groups. Brad was seated in a chair next to a lamp, eating. He was watching the group across the room as they listened to Barry tell one of his many jokes. Whenever Barry talked, people listened. Every two minutes there would be a loud roar of laughter from the group, and it was always after Barry finished his joke.

Sally Harper came up to Brad and sat next to him.

"So what are you doing sitting here all alone?" she asked. "Trying to relax?"

"Actually, I'm quite relaxed."

She put her hand on his arm. "I'm pulling for you on Friday."

"Thanks."

"You excited?"

"Nope."

"No? You should be. You have an excellent chance."

"Thanks."

"Really, you do. Oh, hi Fred." Fred Hartz came over and Sally stood up next to him. "Now here is what I call a relaxed man," said Sally to Fred, referring to Brad.

"Brad is always relaxed," Fred affirmed. He bent down to whisper in Brad's ear. "I'm pulling for you, buddy. Hope you get it."

Brad stood up. "Hope I do too. Thanks, man." He chewed into another cookie as he heard the group around Barry roar another laugh. He noticed Barry had been the only one talking in that group for about fifteen minutes.

"You and Barry came to Gellem at about the same time a few years back, didn't you?" asked Fred.

"Yes, we did. He came in two months after me."

"But Barry started lower, didn't he?" asked Sally. "You were an assistant planner, and he . . . well, hello Janet." She saw Janet come her way. "Excuse me, Brad." Sally left to talk to Janet and Fred followed her, leaving Brad alone again to collect his thoughts.

He went to a counter and got a beer, and then decided to get some fresh air and step outside. On the way out the door he heard another round of laughter around Barry, and the group had gotten larger.

Brad stood next to a fountain holding his beer when Fred joined him.

"So, are you counting the hours now?" Fred asked.

"Wish it were over. As a matter of fact, in forty-eight more hours it will definitely be over." Brad took a drink of his beer.

"The waiting game is hard. Like a wedding ceremony. Say, how's the wife doing?"

"Dierdre is doing fine. She had the flu so bad last week, I thought I was going to have to stay home and watch John. But she got over it quick. That was a major concern."

"Is it hard, trying to do a balancing act between the family and your job?"

"No, not really. The family will always be there, regardless with what happens at work. Say, thanks for bringing up my family. Really, I mean it." Brad looked at Fred with a sincere penetrating look. "Dierdre is always understanding when I need to work late. She knows I need to pay the bills. She's a good thing to come home to." He looked at his watch. "As a matter of fact, I probably should be hitting the road pretty quick."

"Well, drive safely," Fred cautioned. "The Holiday party will be real relaxing for me *this* year. Last year I thought I was in the running to get the senior planner position when Doris left. Didn't get it."

Brad finished his beer. "You'll have your day in the sun one of these times. Well, take care. See you tomorrow at work."

❦   ❦   ❦

Friday morning was bright and cheery in Los Angeles, and the temperature was unusually warm for December. The agency had rented an elaborate hotel ballroom. The party was to begin around ten with an open bar, and most of the employees arrived by ten-thirty. The meeting was not to begin until after eleven.

People began drinking beer and wine as soon as they arrived. Barry loved Chablis, and after three glasses realized he had had too much. He became dizzy and knew that he had to get himself back together before the meeting began, which he hoped would start late.

The meeting started before twelve and was held in a smaller room than the ballroom. It was adjacent to the ballroom and could seat about two hundred, which was the approximate attendance.

All of the executives sat near the front, and there was a podium with a microphone at the front and center. A screen was behind the podium to show the agency's creative work with both the print ads and snapshots of commercials produced during the year.

The meeting started with introductions of the executives, including the ones who had come from New York, the home of Gellem's main office. Barry's palms started to sweat because of the introductions, and the fact he might just become one of the executives in a few minutes. Barry was sitting in the fifth row on the aisle. Brad was near the back, off to the side, and sitting with Sally Harper.

After the introductions and applause, there were film clips of commercials the creative department had done that year for their clients, followed by some graphs and charts of the agency's billings and the clients gained and lost. There was a speech by the chairman of the board on the philosophy of Gellem and Bates, followed by a dignitary from New York who talked a little about profit sharing. Finally, the promotions were to be announced. Knots swelled up in the stomachs of a few people, including Barry and Brad.

Promotions were announced for the creative department, followed by the account group, the production and traffic departments, plus those in human resources. Then an advancement that surprised everyone occurred when mailroom clerk, Bob Gomez, became mailroom supervisor, and with it he would be given two assistants. Bob received the biggest ovation so far. He had been with the company for twelve years and was a very quiet man. Barry could not remember seeing Bob talk more than twice since he joined the agency. But he was well-liked, stayed out of trouble, and did his job extremely well. He was extremely surprised and no one had seen his smile as big as when he shook hands with the announcer of the advancement. The media department was last, and it seemed like an hour of waiting for Barry.

Chuck McDermott, the media director, was called to the mike to announce the promotions for his department.

"From planner to senior planner, Janet Marshall." A round of applause, the action of surprise by the recipient, a kiss or a shaking of the hand (depending upon the gender of the employee), and the presentation of a gift to the newly promoted—this was the general order after each announcement.

"From assistant buyer to senior buyer, Paula Ossen. . . . From media assistant to assistant planner, Bill Davidley. . . ."

"And last but certainly not least," was followed by a gasp of half of the audience. "From senior planner to supervisor, Sally Harper." Sally first gave Brad a hug, and then scurried up to the front. She gave Chuck a bear hug, took the flowers, and waltzed back to her seat.

What happened with the new associate media director position? This was the unanimous thought in the room. The position was open, needed to be filled, and Barry and Brad were the prime candidates. Chuck sat down. Then a member of the board quickly spoke to him. Chuck stood up and walked to the mike.

"It looks like I've forgotten about one other position that needs to be filled," he said rather sheepishly. The audience laughed mildly and sympathetically.

Barry wasn't sympathetic. How in the world could a media director forget such a thing? That was unforgivable, he thought. And I'm sweating bullets. He doesn't know his rear end from a hole in the ground and I'm going to be his associate working under him.

"I will now announce our new associate media director who will also be given the title of Vice-President," said Chuck. "After much deliberation, my final choice is . . . Barry Lord." Chuck was going to say more, but the applause cut him off. Barry immediately got up from his chair, shook a few hands before reaching the front and shook Chuck's hand once.

"Speech!" everyone shouted. "Speech!"

Chuck sat down and Barry stepped up to the mike. The audience became silent.

Barry was beside himself with joy. "Thank you. I'm glad about this honor. Well, I guess age has finally caught up with Chuck. Maybe a year from now he'll forget where his office is and then I can grab it while I direct him to mine," he joked. There was quick laughter, followed by a quick moan. Some in the audience shook their head, but Barry didn't see it because he was smiling at Chuck, who didn't return a smile. "Wouldn't that be something?" The audience was *very* quiet. Didn't they understand his joke, he thought. "To swap places with Chuck someday? Well, it's been a long road, and I'm glad I've seen the light at the end of the tunnel. Thank you." There was some applause. Barry sat down in his seat. The President of the company then adjourned the meeting, mentioning that the bar was open again and there would be music and dancing followed by lunch.

Brad came up to Barry and shook hands, and offered his congratulations. Neither one could think of anything else to say, so Brad walked away.

About an hour later the party was in full swing with loud music, and almost everyone dancing. Even the older generation was getting into the groove. Some of the women in their sixties were rocking and rolling with the younger gentlemen in their twenties. Others were just standing around, holding their wine glasses, playing it cool, occasionally talking to someone. Barry spent most of the time dancing with different girls, and on two occasions saw members of the board staring at him from a distance. He didn't make anything of it, and just continued on having a good time.

He walked to the bar after a break in the music and saw Chuck and Brad standing together.

"Barry," Chuck called out, and motioned for him to come to them.

"Hello Chuck," Barry said cordially. "Hi Brad. Some of those older women I bet are dying to dance with you," he said, looking at Brad.

"Barry, here's our new associate media director," said Chuck straightforwardly, gesturing to Brad.

"The new . . . what. . . ? I don't understand," said Barry.

"It was a perfect set-up and you fell for it," said Chuck. "Barry, we're letting you go, and I think you know why. I didn't really forget to announce who was to be my new associate. I did that on purpose, just to see if you would go to the mike and say something stupid as you did. I got a lot of pressure from the board. I wanted

Brad to be my man all along, but they sort of favored you. I told them the main problem I had with you is your quick mouth before your brain is in gear. I eventually went along with them, but decided to pull a stunt just to see how you would react. You came through as I thought you would. After the meeting, members of the board came up to me and said they now understand what I was talking about."

"But, I was only kidding."

"Of course," said Chuck, nonchalantly. "There are some things you just don't kid about, Barry. If you talk like that about me in front of my face, what are you going to say to people about me when I'm not around? You are to never embarrass your supervisor, and if you talk that way about your boss, you're going to talk like that to the client at a client meeting. Then we lose the account. Then, because we have a reduction in income, we have to lay off hard working employees because there's no money to pay them. All because of your thoughtless, offensive remarks." Chuck was getting louder and pointing his finger at Barry as he spoke. "And the executives will blame me for promoting you. I have a boss too, you know."

Brad just stood there, half of the time looking at Barry and the other half looking at the floor. He had a sympathetic look on his face.

"So anyway, the board members have been coming up to me and telling me to go ahead and do what I think is best. Well, I don't want a guy like you in my department," said Chuck sharply. "You're through, at least in my department. There's an opening for a mailroom assistant now. You may want to try there. Not as much talking is needed." He turned around and asked for some water at the bar, as if his speech was draining him.

Barry didn't know what to say. He turned to walk away.

"Oh Barry, a couple of more things. The advertising agency business is a *very* creative place to work. One of the most creative institutions around. You need to watch yourself if you decide to stay in this business. Not only does this business produce creative ads, but people can find creative ways to make you stay . . . and to make you leave." He looked at Barry intently, but got no facial response. "Secondly, you mentioned in your speech that you finally saw the light at the end of the tunnel. That light was an oncoming car. I'm telling you this because you're in your twenties and still young. Stay on *your* side of the street, and be careful next time."

Barry walked away and headed for the restroom. He was numb and didn't know why he was going there, but felt at the time it was the only place to go. He had to be alone.

"Congratulations, Barry," said someone who passed him and patted his shoulder. He didn't know who it was.

After being in the toilet stall for about ten minutes, Barry came out of the restroom and noticed that the music had softened greatly. Lunch was about to be served. Most of the people were standing around in groups rather than sitting at the tables waiting to be served the meal. Everyone seemed to be talking in the ballroom but him, which was a switch. The word was getting around about his termination, and it would spread like wildfire. He went to the bar quickly to get one last drink before he would leave. While he was waiting for the bartender, he overheard a woman behind him say, "That's two years in a row now. Remember last year when Ellen Tibbs had too much to drink and then she went around to all of the executives to tell them what she really thought of them? She was gone in a flash, and we never saw her again. Now this."

"I know," he overheard a man say. "I can't believe it."

Barry got his drink and gulped it down quickly. He exited from the ballroom as he heard the talking getting louder.

Outside as he descended the steps to get to his car he saw Bob Gomez, the newly crowned mailroom supervisor, ascend the steps. He was going up the steps briskly, as if his joy would almost cause him to fly into the ballroom.

Colette

Jack was looking forward to seeing the family again, although he couldn't understand why when it was his family that had caused the only havoc he had experienced over the last five years. His daughter Colette, age twenty-seven, had gone through a rough marriage and a divorce, one of his sons was an alcoholic, and the other chose to remain aloof from his dad, for reasons that he alone knew and Jack could only speculate. But all three were to meet their father on this warm fall afternoon in Portland at Colette's flat, a meeting that had been planned for months.

The last time the three were together with their dad was at a funeral of their mother two years ago. They had grown up as a close-knit family but when the kids got into their twenties and started making mistakes with their finances, spouses, and careers, the three of them along with their dad started drifting apart. The things that would normally bring a family closer together had caused them to segregate. Jack attributed his one and only heart attack, three years prior, to his older son's financial troubles and the stress it caused him. The younger son's rejection of his father did not help the stress level of his dad either. The sons, Thom and Ray, ages twenty-six and twenty-four, in their younger years would look up to their dad, but when they became more independent after leaving the house, Jack acted as if he hardly knew them. But he continued to enjoy his work as a real estate salesman in the Los Angeles area.

Then there was his daughter Colette. He had never really understood her even when she was a child. They were totally different. Jack would always meticulously finish things he started. He was organized, would think things through before embarking on a task, and complete it the way he wanted. Jack paid attention to detail and would analyze things carefully until he understood the full scope of the situation. Colette was frivolous. She hardly ever finished anything she began; a great starter, and poor finisher. If her chore was to rake the leaves, she would always leave the pile of leaves and not put them in the trash can. If she cooked a meal with everyone sitting at the table, she would always forget something important. One time she prepared a delicious dessert with pie and ice cream and everyone was sitting around the table waiting to begin while she talked for five minutes. Finally Jack got up from the table and got the silverware she had forgotten. Although trying not to let it irk him, it made Jack angry. He had no patience with members of his own family that didn't have the sense to be organized or as astute as he. Colette would make a decision, change her mind the next day, change it back in a couple of days, and become so fickle and flighty that he often wondered how her first husband could have stayed with her as long as he did, and it was only a few months.

Now she was planning to go hastily into another marriage, after knowing the fellow only two months. "But daddy, he's the man of my dreams," she would bellow. Sure, thought Jack. Like the first one. It's time to stop dreaming and wake up. What will you think of him a month from now? Wake up and face the world of reality for once. Jack would have a good talk with her at the reunion.

He arrived at Colette's at about one and everyone seemed glad to see each other, with the customary hugs and trite greetings. Thom and Ray seemed cheerful around their dad, and Jack noticed an air of confidence in Thom. Ray was his normal quiet self, and when he talked he would choose his words very carefully. While the three men were conversing, Colette was making lunch in the kitchen.

They talked about sports, careers, Jack's heart attack, as well as his transition to the single life after his wife's death. They later sat down to eat. Colette remembered the silverware and napkins but forgot the drinks. She ate with them but spent most of the time talking during the meal, using a different subject in her monologue per minute and changing her mind about something relating to the subject every twenty seconds. Jack finally interrupted to tell her that everyone was dying of thirst and at least having some water at the table would alleviate the problem. He got up to help, but Colette told him she would take care of it, and then spent five minutes in the kitchen trying to figure out what would be a suitable beverage.

After lunch, Thom and Ray decided to get in a round of golf at a nearby golf course, if their dad didn't mind. They would be back in the early evening. The family was spending the night together.

"Sure, go ahead. You guys haven't seen each other since the funeral and that was two years ago," said Jack. "You two probably have a lot to talk about, don't you? Enjoy yourselves." He welcomed the idea of having time with Colette alone.

After his sons left, Jack was sitting comfortably eating Colette's apple pie when he notice she was wearing the necklace he had given her many years ago. The necklace had a locket shaped like a heart that could be opened. Out of curiosity, he got up and walked up to her and opened up the locket but found it empty. The locket container was only big enough to hold something like a ring, or perhaps a scrap of paper with a love message on it.

"I'm glad you still like it," he said.

"Why wouldn't I? Of course I still like it," she said effervescently. "Do you remember when you gave it to me?"

Jack showed a blank.

"High school graduation. Remember?"

Jack smiled.

"That was . . . that was ten years ago, daddy. Gosh, did I tell you about the high school reunion we had a few weeks ago?"

Jack didn't like being called "daddy" anymore. Most fathers wouldn't mind, but he did. It made him think of the little girl he still had for a daughter, instead of a woman. He would never be able to tell her he didn't like being called that.

"Yes, you did tell me about your high school reunion," he said. "That is where you met that fellow you plan to marry."

"Oh that's right, isn't it? Yes, he's a great guy. You'll like him. I know you will. He's a sports broadcaster for a minor league baseball team. Roy has a lot of money, and he owns a big sailboat. We plan to get married in just a couple of months and I'm so excited. You know, I don't know why I couldn't have found someone like him earlier when I was about twenty instead of marry that heal who had no concern for. . . ."

"Colette, ah, excuse me, but aren't you rushing this?" her father interrupted with a raised eyebrow. "Do you know very much about him?"

Colette looked stunned, and then re-gathered herself. "Well daddy, of course . . . of course I know lots about him. Why . . . do you think I would ever make a wrong decision or something? Really."

"In your last letter, you described him in great detail and he sort of reminded me of a former boyfriend of yours. Wasn't his name Wade, or something? You were engaged to him and then broke it off."

"No he's not anything like Wade. He's more like . . . like Sam."

"Well, you broke it off with Sam too, didn't you?"

Colette shrugged. "Look daddy, I know what I'm doing, O.K.? I liked Sam, but . . . but we weren't ready to get married then because we were too young. And . . . oh why do I bother telling you these things. You worry too much."

"Why shouldn't I? You're my only daughter, I'm fond of you, and you've made some major blunders and you know it. I just want you to learn from them."

"I have learned from them," asserted Colette, and she got up and went into the kitchen. She got a drink for her father, and then talked to him on matters that had no controversy.

They talked for over an hour. Jack noticed she was not any different than ten years ago.

Why couldn't Colette be stable like her mother, instead of being so fickle?

"I'm enjoying my last job at the furniture store more and more," said Colette, later on. "Next week I will have been there for a whole year. For me, that's really something to be able to stay at one place for a year." Colette grinned as she fiddled with her necklace.

Jack nodded. He himself had worked with the same company for twenty-six years and never thought anything about it.

Thom and Ray came back from the golf game in the early evening, and after dinner all four of them went to a movie. Jack had plenty of time to converse with his two sons, but continued to feel a lack of trust from them when they wouldn't tell him their innermost thoughts about anything. It was all surface stuff. Thom asked his dad for a loan, of course. Jack agreed to it, half way. Ray mentioned very little about his goals, what was happening at work, or his love life. Jack felt a tinge of hurt by this, but had learned over the years to accept the fact that Ray wanted to keep things to himself.

The wedding was two months later. Jack walked Colette down the aisle. He remembered the last time he did this and thought about how wonderful he had felt as he gave his daughter away to enjoy marital bliss that would last a lifetime. Then he saw it blow up in his face. He was hoping for better things this time, but with reality staring at him he couldn't find anything optimistic about what his daughter was getting in to.

At the reception, Thom was getting drunk and loud. Jack had hoped his son was through with his problem with alcohol, but apparently not. He was getting embarrassed and left, as he wasn't needed at the reception anyway. His other son wouldn't say too much to him, and Colette was in another world. He really didn't know anyone else there, as Colette didn't invite any of her dad's friends or business partners to the affair, with the wedding being in Portland.

The marriage lasted only eight months when the divorce papers were filed, and when Colette tried to explain the reasons to her dad over the phone, he didn't want to hear them.

"No. Stop! I don't want to hear anything. I don't want to hear anymore. You don't need to explain anything. Please."

"But daddy, I want to talk to you. I need someone to talk to. Please let me. . . ."

"I don't want to hear anything about it," he said bluntly, and hung up.

Jack was sitting with Thom in a cafe in Los Angeles a few months later.

"I'm really whipping this problem, dad. I've gone three months now with no desire to drink. It's the longest time so far."

Jack nodded. "And you got your promotion just this last week, right?"

"Oh yeah, but that had nothing to do with me whipping the problem. They didn't know about any such problem."

"Oh. Well, that's great news. It looks like things are pulling together for you."

"Dad, you need to talk to Colette. She's troubled that you won't speak to her."

There was silence from Jack.

"I mean, I know she hasn't lived up to your expectations," Thom continued, "and she probably drives you crazy at times, but she really needs somebody to talk to."

"I'll talk to her," Jack responded thoughtfully. "But, I've already told her everything she needs to hear from me. I've been talking to her for years and it does no good. She listens to me, but doesn't do what I say. It's no use. I'm frustrated.

She needs to get her act together. I'm tired of her making these frivolous decisions at the drop of a hat without thinking things through."

"Well, she'll learn as she gets older," said Thom.

"That's what I always thought. I've been thinking that way for years and it hasn't happened. I'm tired of waiting." Jack stopped to think for a moment. "You know, I've been trying to get Ray to open up to me for years and he hasn't, and here Colette opens up too much and says things I've heard so many times I can't stand hearing them anymore. I don't think she'll ever learn."

"Ray is doing well at United Airlines now. He enjoys his work. I miss seeing him. I know he's been dating that girl, what's her name, Lucy. She was at the wedding, do you remember? At Colette's last wedding?"

"Is that the girl with brown hair down to her waist, kind of young in her early twenties, freckles, red lipstick?"

"That's the one. He's been with her now for more than a year. I don't know what's happening. He hasn't really told me."

"Ray never tells me what's happening," Jack said sadly.

"Oh, I need to make a phone call," said Thom suddenly, looking at his watch. "It'll only be a couple of minutes. I'll be right back."

As Jack saw his son walk out to the pay phone, he reflected how things were going better for Thom and how this one was going to turn out all right.

Perhaps he should give Colette a call. She's probably lonely up in Portland. He heard from Thom that her girlfriend moved out on her and got married, so all Colette had was a cocker spaniel to keep her company. And then he remembered that he would only get frustrated again.

It wasn't much more than a year after the divorce was final when Colette was getting married again. It was to be another big ceremony in a church in Portland. She met a thriving young lawyer name Harold. He was totally different than Roy in personality but had the same big bucks. It seemed that all his former and present clients were at the wedding with their families, as well as his lawyer colleagues.

Jack walked down the aisle with his daughter to give her away—again. I feel like an absolute fool, a complete idiot, thought Jack. This is the last time, the very last time.

The wedding went beautifully. It always does, thought Jack. The weddings were always done with class, and everyone was always so confounded happy. And the ladies have to take out their handkerchiefs when the vows are said, as if they've never heard them before at least a hundred times.

The music was always great, and this wedding was no exception. There was a nice and loud reverberating pipe organ, a harp for the prelude, a string orchestra softly accompanying a couple of the solos which were done by what seemed to be operatic performers.

The minister was very eloquent, the candles and flowers were nice, and when the bride and groom were introduced as mister and misses there was thunderous applause as the wedding march from the organ brought an exciting climax to the conclusion of the ceremony. Well all of this nonsense is finally over, thought Jack, as he weathered another one. Then he remembered he was to go to the reception downstairs. He didn't want to disappoint Colette. And he was to toast the couple, or his daughter, or something.

Jack was sitting at a table with Thom, Ray, and a few other people. He learned that Thom was still off of the alcohol except for a few social occasions such as this one where he would drink champagne, and Ray remained aloof to just about everything around him, acting as dull as ever.

Jack had a glass of champagne and then started another, an unusual fete for him. He felt lightheaded and hadn't had that feeling since he was in college. A couple of relatives offered toasts to the entire huge throng and Jack finished his second glass. A few minutes later Colette came up to the microphone.

"I want a certain person to now offer a toast and it is none other than a man that I admire and respect second to none. He is my father. Come up. Come up, daddy." There was applause from the crowd.

Jack had a sense of embarrassment at the announcement. He got up from his chair and staggered. Thom filled his dad's empty glass with more champagne, and Jack walked up to the mike. He looked out and could not remember the last time he spoke to so many. He felt dizzy and had a sense of numbness, as if he couldn't care less what the crowd thought of him or what he was about to say. He wanted to get something off his chest.

"I'm supposed to offer a toast here," he started, and then he realized his voice sounded a little foreign to him. "I'd rather offer a toast to someone I respect, but that is impossible at this point." His words came out elongated and with no sense of rhythm.

The crowd became stony silent. There was a sense of nervousness in the reception hall and there were whispers of "oh no" and "what a shame."

"Harold, you don't know what you're getting into, marrying my daughter, but her first two husbands did and they almost made it through the first year. God bless them, did they ever go through a trip with Colette. She's been more trouble to me . . . well, anyway here's a toast," Jack said as he lifted his glass while everyone else, except for maybe a handful, sat still holding their glasses down. "Here is a toast to you Harold that you won't blow your brains out, and to you Colette, my dear, that you will break with tradition and make it through to the end of that elusive first year of marriage. You'll make it only by our ten thousand prayers, (and who has the time to pray a single prayer for you?), a couple of Red Sea miracles," Jack hiccupped and continued, "and a stroke of luck from some love goddess whose fanning herself and throwing some love darts on planet Jupiter." He hiccupped again, and then drank the champagne, while the crowd watched.

When Jack finished his drink he said thank you to the crowd and took a step forward to go back to his seat when he saw Colette come up to him and throw her glass into his face, with the champagne still in it. The glass cut his cheek bone and there was a big gasp from the people. Colette looked furious, and picked up another champagne glass that was on a nearby table and threw it at his face, hitting him in the eye. Jack covered his face and gropingly tried to find his way back to his chair when he slipped on the champagne that was spilt. His feet gave way beneath him, and as he fell flat on his face, he was cut on the forehead by broken glass on the floor. Blood was spurting out, and before he lost consciousness he heard a few women screaming. Colette yelled, "I hate you!" and someone was yelling, "Stand back! Everyone remain in your seats please!" and it sounded like Thom.

When he regained consciousness, he was in the hospital and nurses were checking the bandages on his face. He saw Thom at the door shaking his head. When he was released, Jack didn't see Thom, or Ray. But his car, with his luggage inside, was left outside the emergency room exit and the nurse gave him his car keys. He drove to the airport and flew back to Los Angeles, talking to no one.

Jack didn't know when the appropriate time would be for him to call Colette. Perhaps there would never be a time. He should actually speak to her in person, and go up to Portland and apologize to both her and Harold. But when he tried calling her to set up a time, she hung up on him immediately. Six months went by, then a year, then two years. No word from Colette.

He thought perhaps he should just go up there without any warning. But if she refused him, or slammed the door in his face, he would be hurt more. He decided to stay in Los Angeles and let time heal the wounds.

Ray came into town and actually dropped by to see his dad.

Jack didn't care if it was for money. He was just glad to see his son. They talked a little about Ray's work at United Airlines, and didn't talk about the incident at the reception. But Jack had to find out how his daughter was doing, and he knew Ray was in contact with her.

"I really want to know," said Jack. "I'm interested. Is she happy? It's been over two years since I saw her. Is she well? How is she doing at the furniture store?"

"I can't tell you," said Ray. "She doesn't want you to know anything about her."

"But . . . is she still married? Has she had a baby? I might be a grandpa and don't know it."

"I can't tell you."

"Why not? I'm her father. I'm her . . . daddy."

"She never wants to speak to you again, dad. Ever. It's over. Nothing can be mended. Let's not talk about her."

"You never talk to me about yourself either," said Jack. "You talk about trite stuff. No depth. You haven't let me get a chance to really know you since you left the house. You won't open up to me." Jack's voice sounded like he was begging. "Why? Why is that? You don't trust me?"

Ray shrugged.

"Thom told me you're moving up at United. That's great. You know, Thom and me get along pretty well now. He's licked alcoholism, and he's doing O.K. at McCann Erickson. Account

Executive. Hasn't found the right girl yet though. What about yourself?"

Ray sighed. It was obvious he didn't want to talk about it.

"I don't think you would want to hear about it," Ray remarked.

"Sure I would." Jack leaned forward. "Come on, tell me, please. Tell me. Please."

"No."

"Why not?"

"All right. I'll go into depth for you, O.K.? I raped one girl and got her pregnant. This was about six years ago, shortly after mom died. She had the baby. She told me if I didn't help financially support the baby that she would go to the police and tell them about the rape. So I had no choice. I have to support the kid. The only reason she didn't report the rape to begin with was because, well, we were going steady at the time and she liked me. She just didn't want to have sex, not at that time. I did, so I forced myself on her . . . and I guess you could say I raped her. After she had the baby we broke up, but she told me I was financially responsible for the kid and told me I had to support the baby or else. In the process of doing that, and losing the job I had at the time, I filed bankruptcy because I had borrowed money and had bills to pay. It was never Thom that had the financial problems, dad. It was me. But I couldn't get myself to ask you for money, so Thom had to pretend he had the problems and ask you for it instead. Whatever money you gave Thom, he gave to me. Get it? Is this going into enough *depth* for you? Let me know when you've had enough depth, all right dad?"

Jack shifted his weight.

"I got into prostitution to work my way out of more financial holes that occurred later. I lied on my application at United to get hired, of course. I got into a car accident three years ago. It was my fault, and I couldn't afford car insurance. It was a Rolls-Royce I hit, of course. They sued me and they're still after me. However much money I save I'm sure they'll try to take from me because I owe them a bundle. Oh, I almost forgot. I was put in jail for a few days shoplifting when I didn't have enough money. You know it's a felony. Thom bailed me out of jail. I lied to my boss at United, telling him I was sick." Ray stopped, and thought for a moment. "Oh, I've gotten two other girls pregnant. Not Lucy, the one you met at one of Colette's weddings, but two other girls. One girl says she's putting the baby up for adoption, and the other is keeping it and marrying somebody else. So I will probably never get to see two of my kids. Never. I've lost track of those two girls. Is this enough opening up for you, dad? Do you want more detail? I suppose if I think hard enough I can tell you more."

"No. That's O.K.," said Jack blandly. He looked sad, and looked down and rubbed his forehead. To realize he was technically a grandpa three times over was enough for one dialogue. "Thank you for telling me these things. I wish you had done it sooner. I still love you regardless." Jack really believed that last statement and he wanted Ray to believe it.

"Things are O.K. at United," Ray said slowly. "But I don't have much drive or incentive, knowing that whatever I make and save will eventually be taken from me by the Rolls-Royce people and of course I need to support that one baby of the girl I supposedly raped."

Jack wound up the conversation quickly. He didn't want to talk anymore. It was depressing him. He and Ray parted, and Jack showed little emotion when Ray drove off.

It was now twelve years later. Jack was in his early seventies, and had not remarried. He was retired from his real estate job and spent a lot of his time traveling and enjoying one of his favorite pastimes, bowling. Jack and Thom were on the best of terms. Thom was married with two children and living in the Los Angeles area, so they saw each other often. Ray lived up in the Portland area, and remained aloof from the rest of the family. All that Jack knew was that Ray was still working for United Airlines and remained single, he thought.

It was at this time that Jack received the phone call telling of Colette's death. She died of a brain tumor. The phone call was apparently from one of Colette's close friends who located members of the family. Jack was so stunned when he heard the news that he couldn't move for a few seconds, and when he did he found himself shaking. A brain tumor at the age of forty-three? He had not seen or spoken to her since the wedding reception, but had not given up hope that one day she would accept him into her presence. Years ago he would make the annual phone call and get hung up on immediately. His letter of apology had been refused and returned, with the envelope unopened. Jack had given up trying on his own, but had hoped that over a period of time she would eventually call on him.

The funeral was held at a church in Portland. Jack recognized the name and address of the church as the same church he last saw her when she married Harold, the lawyer. It was going to be a rough trip to Portland, he thought.

Jack arrived at the church fifteen minutes early. He knew that members of the family would be sitting up front but couldn't find Thom, Ray, or the minister. He decided to walk downstairs to where the wedding reception had been, fourteen years earlier, and remembered the room very well. The room looked very similar, but no tables were set up, and of course, no decorations. He saw where he gave his fateful speech, and realized again that one could not erase and rerecord a part of a person's life. There was no back-space key. Jack had done his best to apologize, and had to leave it at that. There was a custodian sweeping and he came up to Jack.

"Can I help you with anything, sir?" he asked in a kindly manner.

"No thank you. Just looking."

The custodian looked hard at Jack. "Say, haven't I seen you from somewhere? Your face looks familiar for some reason or another. Hmm."

"No I don't think so," Jack said quickly.

The custodian shook his head. "You must be reminding me of someone else then. I can't exactly place you." He went on with his sweeping.

Jack left the reception room. He realized this must have been the same custodian who cleaned up all the mess.

Jack found Thom and Ray in the narthex of the sanctuary. The funeral attendant brought them down to the front pew on the left, and they sat with Thom's wife and children. A man with two children came in and sat in the front pew on the right. Jack looked over there and saw that the man was definitely not Harold, but wondered if the two kids were his dear grandchildren. They sort of had Colette's features, Jack pondered. The dark-haired fellow was, he thought, her latest husband.

What was unusual about the funeral, Jack noticed, was the fact the immediate family of the deceased was not gathered together before the service in a separate location, and then enter the sanctuary as a unit at the beginning of the service and sit together. Instead, the service attendants were telling each family member where to sit in the front. Jack thought it could be because Colette's husband did not want him as part of the family gathering beforehand.

Jack read the printed obituary. No mention of Colette's mother and father in it. There was a mention of her husband Charles, and their two children, Kaitlyn and Jeremy, ages five and three. Jack looked over at them again. He started weeping, but then controlled himself.

The service began. There were a couple of solos, a Scripture reading, and a short speech of Colette's life by the minister. He found out some new things about Colette's life during the speech, but didn't seem to care so much about these facts. Jack only cared about the relationship with his daughter, and as he looked at the closed casket in front of him he knew the relationship was over and there was nothing more he could do. He had walked his only daughter down this same middle aisle at the wedding and remembered how he felt at that time. But he decided to blank those thoughts from his memory.

The service concluded. Jack was surprised when the casket was opened. He was going to see her one last time. The non-family attendees walked up to see her first and then mostly scattered. Then it was the family's turn. Jack wanted to say something to Colette's children and husband, but decided to wait. Thom and Ray saw Colette, and then Jack saw her. She looked like one who had done some suffering, but was now at peace. He noticed she looked very much like her mother did when she was that age.

"Oh Colette," he said softly. He then noticed she was wearing the necklace with the locket that he had given her at the high school graduation about twenty-five years ago. Jack pondered why she was wearing it. Did it really mean that much to her? Bless her. She probably gave instructions to someone before she died to have her wear it.

Jack decided to do what he had done often when she wore it. He reached over to the locket and opened it. To his surprise he saw a wadded up piece of paper. He unfolded it, and it said, "I hate you daddy." Immediately he wadded it back up again and was ready to put it back in the locket. Then he thought maybe he should put it in his pocket and tear it up later. But he thought no. Let her hatred be buried with her. He put it back in the locket and closed it up.

Looking behind him, he noticed that both Thom and Ray had read it. Colette's husband had apparently read it, as well as a couple of bystanders. The first reaction he noticed was from Colette's husband who gave him a stern and hateful look. Charles apparently knew about everything. He walked away taking his two children with him out the side door into a hallway. A bystander shook her head at Jack. Thom was looking the other direction, but he saw Ray looking at him with a somewhat sympathetic look. He had never looked at his father that way before.

Jack took one more look at his daughter and then walked toward the side door. He noticed Thom and Ray following him. Jack wanted to get to his car quickly, and didn't want to talk to anyone. But when he went through the door he saw Colette's children in the hallway standing next to their father who was talking to someone. His grandchildren looked adorable, and yet they looked somber because of the event, with uncertainty in their eyes because they couldn't fully understand what had really happened to their mother. Jack wanted to talk to them and tell them who he was. He wanted to help them. A drink at the drinking fountain gave him more time to think, and he heard in the background Charles talking about how much Colette suffered and how the brain tumor happened so quickly.

Jack finished drinking, then turned around and was ready to approach his grandchildren when Colette's husband stopped talking and noticed Jack and gave him a look of disdain. Had Jack tried to talk to Kaitlyn and Jeremy at that time, he believed Charles would have punched him out, based on the fiery gaze that was in his eyes. He walked down the hallway and out into the parking lot towards his car.

"Dad!" he heard from behind him. Thom walked briskly up to his dad, and Jack stopped. Thom put his arm around Jack and hugged him.

"I'm sorry dad," Thom said simply, and began crying. Jack had never seen him weep as an adult.

He saw Ray, out of the corner of his eye, walk to his car. Ray would drive off and not say anything to his dad, and if he had it wouldn't have been much more than how are the tomatoes growing in the back yard, or how is the bowling game. Jack knew at that moment, beyond a shadow of a doubt, that his relationship with Ray would mend. Things would be fine, someday. But the time was not now. It would be a future time, cut in stone. The time at hand was with Thom.

Jack continued to feel Thom's arm around him and the moisture of the tears on his shoulder as they embraced. Someone could understand his feelings, could sympathize, and see beyond outward appearances, and he began to cry as well. The trip to Portland and the funeral had been worth it. The negative experience with Colette and the locket had been balanced by Thom's love for his dad, and he knew it was there permanently.

Thom's wife, Sally, and their two children, Matt and Stephen, ages ten and eight, were standing by their rental car watching father and son embrace.

"I'm going with dad to have a talk, honey," Thom told Sally. "I'll meet you at the hotel in about an hour."

"Sounds good," she said. "Come on guys, get in the car."

Jack looked over at his grandsons. "Say, Matt, Stephen. Did you bring the football?"

The boys nodded, with anticipation.

"Later on this afternoon, let's all go to a park and throw the football around, and the Frisbee. Would you like that?"

Matt and Stephen jumped with glee and gave off a shout before they got in the car.

Thom conversed with his father a little more after his family drove away, then got into Jack's car and they would go to the nearest cafe and talk for a long time.